ALSO FROM DARK TIDINGS PRESS

THE GODS AND MEN CYCLE

By Kristopher Jerome

The Broken Pact Trilogy:

- Wrath of the Fallen
- Cries of the Forsaken
- Tears of the Godless

The Nightbreaker

White Wings from Grey Ash

Before the Breaking:

- A Bandit's Balance
- A Voice from the Darkness
- In the Shadow of Light
- The Sons of Lighthammer
- The Bard's Demons
- Disciples of the First Cycle
- Ten of Seatown
- The Last Gift of Kane Darksend
- The Grey God's Edict
- The Blood-Soaked Sacrament

BACKWOODS GRINDHOUSE

By Kristopher Jerome

She Who Sleeps Beneath the Trees

Dolls From the Woods

They always get the
likeness right.

DOLLS FROM THE WOODS

KRISTOPHER JEROME

Paperback ISBN: 978-1-951138-22-6

For Mom,
Who thinks she knows where all of the bodies are
buried.

ON THE LAST EPISODE
OF BACKWOODS
GRINDHOUSE

Podcaster Treyton Savage comes to the town of Jackson Point to get information on an active serial killer. He quickly learns that something deeper is wrong with the quaint little town; no one can leave, and time acts much differently here.

With the help of his new friends, Kevin Anderhoff, Samantha Moore, and Rebecca White, Trey uncovers a cult that worships an ancient being known as the Rootmother. In an act of desperation, Trey commits suicide, but awakens back in his bed the next day.

The murders are an attempt by the cult to awaken the Rootmother and usher in the end of the world. After Kevin becomes the latest sacrifice, the rest of the group searches the abandoned Ansel Mansion for a clue as to how to destroy the creature responsible for the killings. They discover a journal that claims the monster can be killed with fire.

The mayor, Arthur Tench, and his cousin, the sheriff, Nancy Tench, explain the history of the town and the plans of the cult—known as the Fifth Signet—to the group. They plan to strike at the cult leadership, composed mostly of the city council, when they inevitably come for the mayor as the final sacrifice.

Though the mayor is killed, the final sacrifice is actually Becca, who is kidnapped and taken to the Elder One's Crown, a collection of mysterious stones that are supposedly part of the Rootmother herself. Trey and Sam save Becca and destroy the monster, who turns out to be Sam's boyfriend, Gideon Nelson.

Trey and the cult agree to a temporary truce following the events, as each side holds significant leverage against the other. Finally, Trey accepts that he is stuck in Jackson Point and decides to start a new podcast exploring his encounters with the Elder Ones titled *Backwoods Grindhouse*...

DOLLS FROM THE WOODS

1

A mighty pine fell in the distance, causing a crack like thunder to split the air. Henrietta Frock still hadn't gotten used to the sound. She had been in the logging camp-turned-town of Jackson Point for only a few odd weeks. Her husband, Willard, had taken a job here, bringing his little family with him from back east.

While the air was fresh here—fresher than the slums of Boston where she had grown up, at least—the ground felt *wrong*. Whenever she or her boys dug in it, their hands burned. Sometimes, maggots and other grubs would be writhing about on their doorstep like they were atop some carcass. Their dog had gone rabid, too, likely bitten by a raccoon or some other vermin that roamed the woods. Willard had shot the poor thing just last week. Henrietta hated it here. Still, it was where their money was coming from, at the moment.

A millionaire by the name of Frederick Ansel has brought all manner of folks to the camp to clear the forest and provide some of the best lumber to the Oregon Territory. Then he died. Now Jackson was a mess of conflicting interests and squabbling old folks who wanted to run everything. The sawmill continued on, though, under the control of the Tench family.

It was Augustus Tench, the current patriarch of the family, who had decided to recruit loggers and sawyers from the eastern United States to staff the mill. While Willard had believed this was simply because they worked harder where they had come from, Henrietta had started to think it was actually because the locals knew something was off about this place.

The rumor was that Ansel had been murdered last year, after all. And before that, bodies were found chewed up in the woods. Even so, the work continued, and most paid the violence no mind. Trees grew quicker and stronger here. Because of her, they said. The Green Goddess. Henrietta didn't take stock in such heathen nonsense, as that was the provenance of Indians and Catholics.

Another tree landed with a resounding boom that shook the shutters on the Frock house. Henrietta sighed and continued hanging the laundry outside. Her boys, Joshua and Ezekiel, played between saplings a few yards away, trading off which boy was the logger and which was the tree monster. She didn't much like this game, but it kept them out of her hair while their father worked.

"Tell the bitch of the bark I'm coming for her!" Joshua shouted.

"Joshua Frock, what did I tell you about that kind of language?!" she scorned.

"Sorry, ma!" he laughed. "It won't happen again."

It was sawyers' talk, that was. The men who spent most of the time inside the sawmill, rather than out felling the trees, put much less stock in the legends about the Green Goddess. While Henrietta appreciated that the men her husband worked with directly were good, God-fearing men, she could have done without their crude talk, especially in front of the children.

Across the muddied path from their house sat a little cottage that had been empty since the Frocks had gotten there. Now, a carriage pulled to a stop, and a family clambered out, five of them in all. The wife, a waifish thing that Henrietta would've figured for a girl rather than a woman-grown, waved at her meekly. Their children, a little girl who seemed to be just weaned, and two boys close to her sons' ages, immediately ran around the cottage, whooping and hollering like they were having the most fun they had ever had in their lives. Each of them had a shock of raven-colored hair the likes of which she hadn't seen before.

The husband, though, seemed to be a dour sort. He was gaunt himself, with sunken eyes and a thick mustache that he waxed into two thick points. He carried a briefcase that looked large enough to fit one of their children in. Once he was out of the carriage, he didn't give either Henrietta or the rest of his brood a second glance before he went inside. A few minutes later, he was back out, sour-faced as ever.

"This won't do," he said to the driver. "I specifically demanded a house, not some ramshackle hut like this. And I made it especially clear that I was to have a cellar. Is there another more suitable property, or will I need to speak to Tench myself?"

"I'm sorry, sir," the other man said, bowing low. "I believe the mistake is mine. There is a house in the forest that Mr. Tench said was reserved for a member of The Fifth Signet. That must be the one you were promised?"

The man's face grew even darker, and for the first time, his eyes fell on Henrietta. She tried to look busy again, hanging the clothing with more vigor than before.

"I thought you were told," he whispered sharply, though his voice still carried, "not to mention that name in public. Tench may run the town, but that name heard by the wrong ears could lead to disaster."

"My apologies, Mr. Winslow," the driver said, bowing even lower than before. "I had forgotten to be discreet. It shan't happen again."

"Well, get in!" Winslow snapped at his family.

Just as they had climbed out in a rush, so too did they clamber back inside. Then the carriage was off, leaving Henrietta alone on the street. She thought them odd, but aimed to pay them no mind, until something glinting in the afternoon sun caught her eye. Lifting her skirts, she trotted across the mud and picked up a small China Doll. It looked like a little girl, not unlike the Winslow child. Her face wasn't smiling, though, but seemed to be moaning in pain. The thing gave her an uneasy feeling; even so, she dropped it into one of her dress pockets and intended to return it to them once Willard got home. It was the neighborly thing to do.

The house that the Winslow patriarch had finally settled on was a small manor deeper into the forest than Henrietta was willing to walk. After asking around for which home the new family had taken, she was able to borrow a horse from Edward Phillips down the road and made her way into the woods just as the sun was starting to set. Normally, she would never have been out this late, but something inside bid her to return the doll to them.

A pathway had been cleared through the trees here—she didn't dare call it a proper road—which led into the forest where some of the larger homes had been built as of late. Henrietta couldn't have imagined living this far from the mill. Who knew what kinds of wild animals stalked these trees after nightfall?

The horse she rode looked to be an old mare, not far from being unable to make such a trek. But if Edward was to be believed, this horse was only six years old. The poor thing was a far cry from Megara, whom she raised since she was a filly. Megara had broken a leg and died shortly before they moved to Jackson Point. Henrietta was almost grateful now that she lived in the place. Something here was no good for the animals.

The swaths of trees that loomed over her on each side finally cleared out in a semicircle. The path continued on into the shadows of the wood, but off to the left, there now sat a large house, nearly double the size of the one the Winslows had inspected in town. Kerosene lamps glowed faintly from inside the front windows, a sign that night was nearly here.

Henrietta hopped off the mare and walked up to the white lacquered door with the doll clutched tightly in her hands. She hoped that the Winslow man wouldn't be the one to answer. She didn't have any desire to see him again.

RAP RAP RAP.

Her knuckles struck the door, softer than she had intended. Something about this place had set her on edge. *It was just the thought of being in the woods after dark*, she told herself. Though the word *Rootmother* seemed to loom in her mind like a specter, she refused to acknowledge.

After a short time, the door opened a crack, spilling the amber light of the lamps onto the porch. Thank the Lord it was the wife who peered out, and not the husband.

"May I help you?" the woman asked in a tremulous voice.

"Yes!" Henrietta said too loudly. "My name is Henrietta Frock. I live in town, actually across the street from the house you inspected earlier. After you left, I found this in the road."

She shoved the doll forward in a jerky fashion.

Her nerves had truly gotten the better of her. What would her mother think to see her acting so rudely to a lady who appeared to be of a wealthy disposition? The woman took the doll, her expression flitting between sadness and a forced smile.

"Thank you, Mrs. Frock," she said with a curtsy, "I can't believe we didn't notice that we lost Winifred."

She tucked the doll inside the door somewhere out of sight before opening it wider.

"Would you like to come in for a moment?" the woman asked.

Henrietta considered denying the request so that she could be home before dark, but she decided that she needed to make up for her prior rudeness.

"Why yes, thank you."

She followed the woman into the small foyer, where crates and parcels of various sizes looked to have been recently stacked. While they had obviously just taken residence in the house this afternoon, she hadn't thought about the actual act of moving in and unpacking, not for a family of their apparent means, in any case.

"Forgive the clutter," the woman said, as if reading Henrietta's mind. "I'll need a few days to get the house sorted, I'd expect. Oh! Forgive my rudeness! My name is Eliza Winslow."

Henrietta smiled and gave Eliza a small nod. She was just glad that she wasn't the only one who had forgotten propriety in the moment. Eliza led Henrietta out of the foyer and into what appeared to be a future dining room. An ornate cherry table was already in place, with some ten chairs seated around it.

"Expecting lots of guests from Jackson Point?" Henrietta asked, silently chastising herself for once again being too forward.

"Why yes, in fact!" Eliza said with some glee. "Hyrum says that he has many friends in this community already. The boys and I were stunned, to tell you the truth. Ever since…well, let's just say that my husband likes his own company the best."

"What does Hyrum do, if you don't mind me asking? This seems an awfully nice home for a sawyer or a logger."

Eliza's smile vanished, and her eyes flitted around the room. Then they fell back on Henrietta, and her smile returned, large as ever.

"Hyrum is a dollmaker! You brought some of his handiwork with you tonight, in fact. He is unmatched in the crafting of porcelain."

A loud thump from overhead gave both women a start. Then the sound repeated, followed by laughter and the thunderous sound of boys running down a hall. Eliza shook her head in mock disapproval.

"My boys," she sighed. "Alastor and Malthus. Do you have any children, Henrietta?"

"I have two boys myself, Joshua and Ezekiel."

"Good, biblical names," Eliza said wistfully. "After Winifred, Hyrum chose the names of our children. Heaven knows where he got them from."

"And what's this?" a male voice boomed.

Henrietta spun around to see Hyrum Winslow, stripped down to his undershirt and breaches, glowering at the pair. The man was greasy and covered in sweat, no doubt from moving crates and other things about the house. His expression was even harsher now than it had been earlier that day.

"Hyrum," Eliza said meekly, "this is Henrietta Frock. She found Winnie in the road and brought her all the way here. Wasn't that kind of her?"

"Aye," the man said, though his face never softened. "And now that's done, you best be on your way."

"Of course, don't want to be out after dark," Henrietta said with a curtsy.

"Let me walk you out," Eliza said.

"No need," Hyrum growled. "I'll do it."

Henrietta felt the hairs on her neck prickle.

In the light of lamps, the man's thin face looked almost skeletal. Even in silence, his mustache seemed to quiver with rage. Once on the porch, he grabbed Henrietta by the arm and pulled her close enough that she could smell the stink of dirt on him. She tried to protest, but he held a grimy finger over her mouth.

"I'd prefer if you didn't come to my place of residence again," he whispered. "It's not safe in these woods for a woman."

Then he turned and slammed the door without another word. Henrietta climbed onto the old mare and urged it back into town as quickly as it was able. She gave the Winslow house one final glance before it was swallowed by the trees.

A silhouette from one of the upper windows watched her go.

2

Research into how I can get out of Jackson Point has slowed these last few weeks. I've started a new job that will hopefully allow me to get some nuggets of intel about the Elder Ones or the Fifth Signet that I can share with you all soon. Keep the emails coming, I am desperate to connect with others who have experienced similar events. This is Treyton Savage, and you've been listening to Backwoods Grindhouse.

Trey ended to recording and leaned back into his chair. He wasn't happy with this episode. Nor had he been happy with the last several. After relating the story of what had happened those few months ago when he had first come to Jackson Point, he had quickly run out of material. At this point, he was just recycling old content from *The Dead and the Undead* through the lens that some of the cases he previously covered were actually connected to the higher beings known as the Elder Ones.

The feedback hadn't been great. While Kevin Anderhoff had made those connections while listening to Trey's previous show, anyone else who hadn't lived through what Trey had thought it was all nonsense and the podcaster had finally jumped the shark. Most of the emails that he had received after launching the new show had bemoaned the ending of the previous one, and called him out for a fraud. Some thought he was just doing some tongue-in-cheek fiction podcast masquerading as True Crime as part of its shtick. Very few took his words seriously at this point, which felt deflating.

Now that he had another weak episode in the can, he would sit on it for a few days before editing it and uploading it to the web. He needed another angle, and soon, or else this idea was going to fizzle out and he was going to be stuck here with no further lifeline to the outside world. His family and friends had thought he had gone off his rocker when he told them that *yes,* he had dropped everything to move into the middle of nowhere, *no,* he couldn't ever leave to see them—even for the holidays, and *under no circumstances* were they to try and visit him.

Trey had enough guilt tugging at him already. He didn't need to draw another fly into the web that was Jackson Point. He looked at his phone and saw that it was nearly 8:30 AM. Samantha had been gone for an hour already, which had given Trey the best environment to record his podcast. He stood up from his chair, pulled some sweats on over his boxers and went to the kitchen to get a beer from the fridge. His shift didn't start for another six hours or so, which meant he could get a few beers in and still not get fired.

Samantha's house was quiet while she was away. That made it decent for audio recording, and hell on his nerves the rest of the time. He missed her and Becca both when they weren't around; they made him feel safe. Living with an attractive woman and spending most of his time with another would have excited him not six months ago, but now it was practically torture. Though they had all grown very close, none of them were willing to cross the line from friend to lover yet.

Sam was still mourning Gideon in her way, and Trey and Becca...had some similar nocturnal dispositions that kept either of them from doing anything physical. Trey figured that he would need to buy a new set of sheets soon. The blood stains weren't coming out anymore…

He plopped down on the couch and thumbed through the book on the coffee table. Some shitty horror paperback that Becca had dropped off for him. It was cute that she kept bringing him books that he claimed he liked, but he hadn't actually had the stomach to read them in some time. Trey took a long pull from the bottle before setting it on the table. This was going to be another long-ass day.

Trey tried to shake the cloudiness of the beer from his head as he started his midmorning jog. The early morning February mist was finally starting to snake its way back underground. Not for the first time, he thought of the Rootmother inhaling and exhaling from her slumber deep under the town.

Khythk'uhn.

Her true name burned his mind like a brand. Whenever he thought of it, he couldn't shake it loose for hours, it seemed. It was like even thinking of it caused her to take notice of him. *No wonder Tench didn't like to hear me say it,* he thought. The gunshot thundered, and his ears started buzzing again, just like when he had shot and killed Arthur Tench back in October. The bloody wound blossomed on the man's shirt like a rose. BOOM! Another retort of the revolver, and Clinton Abner was falling in front of him, the principal's dark robes mercifully obscuring most of the damage.

Trey couldn't force the images from his mind, no matter how hard he tried. Even though Tench had been alive the next day, up and walking around like nothing had happened, Trey had still killed him. Trey had still taken the life of an innocent man. The fact that time had returned Arthur Tench, for a short while at least, didn't absolve Trey of his guilt. Just like the fact that he was breathing now didn't change the fact that he himself had died.

The car sped into the tree. Trey flew through the windshield. His head struck a branch and tore from his shoulders, leaving a ragged and bloody lump at the tree's roots. He stared at the sky, unblinking for several moments before his synapses quit firing.

When he realized what was happening, Trey found himself sitting on a bench, covered in a cold sweat. The nightmares were bad, but the daytime flashbacks were worse. He found that he could hardly think about the events of last October without reliving some part of them. Sam said he had PTSD. Unfortunately for him, there wasn't a therapist in the world who would understand what he had gone through, so he had to suffer alone.

No, not alone, he thought, shaking the darkness away. Becca knew what it was like. She carried Jenni with her every day. *And Sam and I have Kevin.* Jackson Point looked like a living town, but in truth, it was just one giant graveyard. One in which not everyone had accepted that they were dead yet. A woman jogged past without giving him a second glance. Trey watched her breasts bounce for a few moments before standing on shaky legs and getting back to his jog.

Forest's Hope Church loomed above Trey. While he held no particular animosity toward the building itself, he certainly disliked its occupants. Forest's Hope held an odd blend of Christianity and paganism, all while worshiping something far older than humanity itself. It didn't help that the Priest, Shepherd Cabot was a member of the Fifth Signet, the cult that worshiped the Elder Ones and sought to bring about the end of the world.

Trey tried not to chuckle. It all sounded like the plot of one of those shitty novels that Becca kept bringing him. No wonder his quickly dwindling listener base thought that he was trying to emulate *The Blair Witch Project* or something. If he hadn't lived it, he wouldn't have believed it himself. He *hadn't* believed it, in fact, until he had died and come back.

He cast a wary glance down Christ's Cross toward the little house where Shepherd Cabot resided. The church itself was currently dark, which meant that Treyton was likely safe for what he was about to do next. Rounding the great building, he jumped the small wrought-iron fence and landed in the smaller of the town's two graveyards.

Picking through the rows of small, unadorned headstones, Trey finally found what he was looking for. Nearly in the center of the graveyard sat a much newer grave, its marker not yet discolored by the elements. Trey knelt in front of it and bowed his head. The marker read: Kevin Anderhoff, beloved son and loyal friend. Tears welled up in Trey's eyes, but as he was alone, he didn't feel the need to brush them aside. It was Kevin's fault that Trey was stuck in this godforsaken place, but it was Trey's fault that Kevin was dead. Another kid sacrificed to the Rootmother like so many before him. Kevin had just been a kid—a kid who wanted to avenge his dead friend and save his town from a cycle of violence. Now he was nourishing the roots of Jackson Point.

Kevin's grandmother had pulled some strings to have the boy buried here instead of in Manifest Destiny, the town's larger cemetery. Trey hadn't been welcomed at the service, and he didn't like to be seen at the graveside either, but he still came often to pay his respects. Kevin's death never should have happened, and Trey swore that he would never let someone die because of him again.

He pulled out his phone and checked the time. 11:33. Just enough time to jog home and grab one more beer before work.

3

Trey walked into the Lodge Tavern at 1:45, fifteen minutes before his shift behind the bar started. The owner, Jameson Stark, was one of the few business owners in town who didn't sit on the city council—and was, presumably, not in the cult. That was why Trey got a job here. That and the hope that he could get locals to open up to him about the strange goings on around town. So far, that hadn't panned out.

He walked into the back room and straightened his glasses in the small mirror beside the time clock. He grabbed a rag, punched in, and headed back into the bar. Cindy was wiping down tables and getting things ready before she left for the night. She had originally done the busier shifts before Trey started. Then someone got handsy with her and Jameson had thrown the bastard out. Now she worked mornings to be safe, and Trey split his tips with her each shift. Cindy turned and gave Trey and small wave before bending back over the table she was furiously working to get the sticky residue of beer off of.

Trey checked all of his taps and took a mental inventory of all of the hard alcohol levels. He didn't expect that he'd have to replace anything on a Wednesday night in February. When Cindy was done, she came over and sat on one of the barstools across from him, her red curls framing her face like a flaming halo.

"Not a soul in here this morning," she relayed with a yawn.

"Not much last night either," Trey said. "That normal for this time of year?"

"Oh yeah," Cindy said, looking at the fresh grime under her nails. "Jameson used to just work the winter months with me and hire on somebody seasonal before the summer. Still not sure why that changed."

She gave him a sly wink. Trey swallowed hard. He didn't like standing out in this town, not anymore. Still, he knew Cindy didn't mean anything by it. She was just playful, and he was an easy target, being the shell-shocked outsider and all. Trey pulled out his wallet and passed

Cindy a measly $20. She grimaced as she put the money into her pocket.

"Slim," she sighed. "Alright, well, I'm getting the hell out of here. Carrie and I have a date at Fernando's later. See ya!"

She hopped the bar and beelined for the back to clock out. Cindy's girlfriend Carrie was a nice girl; she'd been a regular at the library when Becca worked there. The two still chatted about books whenever they found themselves in the Lodge at the same time—usually each to visit one of the two bartenders. Trey knew that he wouldn't see Becca tonight. She had visited him last night, and she rarely came two nights in a row when she was working.

After her old boss attempted to sacrifice her to Khythk'uhn, Becca decided that working at the library would produce a hostile work environment, so she got a new job at Bridgette's Boutique, the only clothing store in town. Somehow, she still got her hands on all of the books she wanted. Trey wondered if Carrie had something to do with that.

An hour ticked by. Then another. Nobody came in. It was just Trey in the front and Jameson snoring in his office until something needed cooking in the back. They hadn't had a cook since he had gotten pulled into the lake or some bullshit. Trey decided not to ask. He wanted to find out everything about the town that he could, but he knew better than to shit where he ate.

Finally, the bell chimed, and one of the regulars, a man named Ace, waddled in. Ace sat at his usual booth and nodded at Trey. Moments later, the bartender was sliding a fresh pint of the cheapest lager that they carried to the man. He would likely drink three or four more of these before closing out and heading home. He never sat with anyone, never brought anything to read or do, never really did anything but stare at the middle distance between his booth and the bar. Trey was pretty sure that the guy worked at the mill, but he never bothered to ask.

So much for getting information out of people at my new job, he thought sourly.

By the evening, the bar had a handful of people in it. Most of them he knew, none of whom were any good at conversation. Certainly not with the guy they still considered an outsider and a troublemaker. The smell of fries and overdone burgers wafted to the front. Jameson was hard at work cooking what passed for food in this place. Trey tried to keep his mind from wandering too much and tried to lose himself in his work. Each pour was harder and harder to hand over to the patrons. It would be a long night before he got to have some himself.

Sometime later, after Trey had clocked out for his break and eaten a blackened hockey-puck of a burger, a new face walked in the door and sat at the bar. The man had dark skin and darker hair. His face had deep lines, and Trey saw when he was waved over that the man's hands were rough from hard work in the mill. It wasn't often that one saw a Native American around this town, though Trey knew there was a family or two.

"What can I get ya?" Trey asked with his best chipper voice.

"The best firewater you've got," the man replied.

Trey stopped short. He was sure that his mouth was hanging open. The man started laughing to himself before he continued.

"I'll take whatever stout is on tap," he said.

"Alright," Trey replied, slowly filling a pint.

"Had you there, didn't I, kid?" the man asked.

"You did. I uh—"

"Didn't know what was more racist, giving me whiskey or asking me if I was serious?"

"Something like that," Trey said, sliding the beer to the man.

"You might have gotten the land, but we get to take your money with the casinos and make you uncomfortable with our jokes. It's not a fair trade by any means, but I do like watching you white boys squirm."

Trey tried to laugh, but he knew that his cheeks were turning red.

"What, never talked to an Indian before?" the man asked.

"I—"

"Jesus Christ, kid, lighten up. You look like you've seen a ghost. Though I'm sure that's normal for you."

Then the man started nursing his beer and paid Trey no further interest. Trey went around to the other scattered patrons, but kept eyeing the newcomer as he did so. He wasn't sure if it was some kind of white guilt or what, but he was determined to make a better impression on the man. Eventually, when the stout was nothing more than foam in the bottom of the glass, Trey returned to try again.

"Some more firewater for you?" he asked with a smirk.

The man didn't smile back.

"Do I need to talk to Jameson about you?" he asked.

Trey shrank down like a deflated balloon.

"Fuck sake, I said lighten up," the man said, laughing again. "I'll do an IPA this time. Leave the jokes to me, though, okay? You suck."

Trey nodded and gave the man his beer, but didn't leave this time. After a few minutes of the customer not acknowledging him, Trey cleared his throat and stuck out his hand.

"I'm Treyton Savage," he said.

"You're kidding," the man replied. His genial disposition seemed to be genuinely melting away.

"No, I...oh..." Trey swallowed again, wishing he could hide under the bar. "That's my actual name, not a racist joke..."

In a flash, the man's smile returned, and he took Trey's shaky hand.

"I knew who you were, kid, that's why I wanted to fuck with you so bad. You might be the only newcomer in town—certainly the only one who caused such a ruckus and got his ass beat in front of the church. Name's Malcolm Bryant."

Malcolm's grip was firm, but his smile was disarming. Trey felt some of his embarrassment and uneasiness melt away. When the handshake was done, Trey leaned in closer as if the two men were conspiring.

"So, Malcolm, your family must have lived around here a long time, yeah?" he asked. "You see, I'm trying to learn everything I can about Jackson Point, so I can...educate people about what's really going on here."

Malcolm started laughing again. Then he drained his beer and pulled out his wallet.

"Look kid, this ain't some shitty movie where the Indian gives sage wisdom to the white man about the powers he doesn't understand. I know about as much as you do about the weird shit that goes on in this place. My ancestors knew better than to come near here. It was you idiots who decided to move in."

"But you're here now?" Trey said, puzzled.

"I am, and that's got nothing to do with your questions. Have a nice night."

Malcolm left cash on the counter and walked back out the door. Trey wasn't sure if he had made a new friend or not.

4

Ron stepped into the Lodge and sat down at the bar. He was planning on having just one quick beer before his next delivery. Though one often turned into two or three. Not that it mattered, the sheriff's department was still in disarray since Tench vanished, so nobody was likely to pull him over tonight.

Assuming they even got another order. It was Wednesday after all. Ron worked for Qik Bite as the delivery driver, which meant that he usually just fucked off for six hours a night and drove around delivering pizzas for the other two. Carl, the shift manager, didn't care what Ron did between deliveries so long as he was back as soon as a call came in.

Before sitting down, Ron smoothed out his greasy black work shirt and ran his hands through his wispy blond hair. Trey was working behind the bar tonight. Ron liked him all right, for an outsider. After the bullshit he stirred up last year, the guy had settled in and nearly become a local. Besides, if the rumors were true, he was banging Samantha Moore *and* Becca White. Not too bad for a newcomer. Ron hadn't even had so much as a handjob in six weeks. His normal hookup, Mary Thorne, had gone missing. She had been talking about leaving, so Ron figured she had slit her wrists and bled out in some motel bathroom in Portland by now.

"Usual, Ron?" Trey asked.

"Yup," Ron said, his voice raspy from his last cig.

The bartender slid a cold lager in front of him. Ron stared at the condensation on the glass for a few moments before he chugged it down and flagged Trey over for another. This wasn't going to be a good night for him; he had decided already.

Fucking dumb bitch, he thought.

His mind wandered back to Mary again. They had been high school sweethearts once. Then Mary had gotten into drugs to cope with the shittiness of living in this town, and Ron had done the same by drinking. Most people in town coped with some vice or another; they just didn't talk about it much. Things had still gone alright between the two of them until Ron caught Mary sucking some other guy off for a dime bag and slapped her around. After that, he only got the occasional action from her when she needed money.

By the time Trey returned with a fresh beer, Ron's mood had completely soured. He had been on a nearly two-week bender with work. For some damn reason, the Rootmother wouldn't let him make it to the fucking weekend. Hopefully, tomorrow would miraculously be Saturday. If not…well, there was always the Lodge.

Ron got Trey's attention to ask, "Where's Cindy?"

Trey seemed to bristle a moment before flashing a dumb smile on his stupid, round face.

"She's not working nights for a bit. People… got a little too familiar with her, if you catch my drift."

"Figures. Nice piece of ass and some idiot always has to take it too far so the rest of us don't even get to see it anymore."

Trey leaned in close enough that Ron could smell that he had been drinking too.

"Don't say something stupid, Ron. Jameson will throw your ass out. Do something stupid, and I'll do something stupid."

"Like what, *outsider?*" Ron asked.

Trey tensed for a moment, his hands gripping

the bar. Then he relaxed, and that dumb smile was back. He adjusted his glasses and started walking away.

"Let me know if you need another one, Ron," Trey called over his shoulder as he disappeared into the back.

Ron sat back, satisfied. *Scared him off*, he thought. *I'm still not one to fuck with around here.* Maybe instead of stopping with his next beer, he'd celebrate with a fourth. They weren't getting another call tonight. It was nearly closing time. Then the phone behind the bar started to ring, and his heart stopped. Nobody called the Lodge. Why the fuck would they?

Trey reemerged and answered the phone with a chipper tone.

"The Lodge Tavern," he said, followed by a long pause. "Yeah, he's here. I'll close him out and send him on his way."

Ron pulled out his wallet as he muttered expletives to himself.

❁

Qik Bite was empty when Ron pulled back into the parking lot. They officially closed in fifteen minutes, leaving an hour for the cleanup shift. He sighed as he got out and pushed his way inside. The building was a squat little thing, with wall-to-wall windows on three sides. Sitting on the counter already were two steaming pizza boxes. Carl was tapping his fingers on top of them with clear agitation.

"You weren't home," Carl said dumbly.

"You found me anyways," Ron replied.

"How many have you had?"

"Just two since you interrupted me. Where do I have to go? I want to get this over with."

Carl sucked on his teeth for a moment before answering. "Some place way out Wacum Road. I've got the address on the box."

Ron clenched and unclenched his fists.

"That far this late? Who the fuck are these people?" he asked.

"Customers," Carl said. "Now get them their fucking pizzas so we can all go home."

Ron grabbed the boxes and stormed back out the door. Of course, it had to be way out in the goddamned woods at this time of night. Even he didn't have enough of a death wish to speed down those winding country roads after dark. Who knew what could jump out at you?

Throwing rocks up behind him, Ron chirped his tires and peeled out of the parking lot, giving Carl the finger for good measure. Maybe he didn't need this job? Maybe he followed Mary and punched his ticket somewhere north of here.

Who wanted to die in this fucking place anyhow?

If you're lucky enough to stay dead, he thought.

Soon, he was swinging out Wacum Road, and the trees swallowed the faint light of the town behind him.

The forest was darker than usual. At least, Ron thought so. Most of his deliveries were in town and took a whopping five minutes from start to finish. Every once in a while, though, he got stuck with this bullshit. Wacum Road held some of the larger houses in the area, though most of them were run down and looked abandoned.

Each clearing of trees either showed a house or a mailbox at the mouth of a smaller dirt road. He eyed the numbers uneasily, trying to gauge how far he actually had to go. It seemed like this address would be so far out that he would end up wrapping around the mountain and back down to the freeway.

Then he found it.

It was a giant, looming thing, with broken windows and a rusted-out car on the front lawn. He pulled into the gravel driveway and whistled quietly to himself. Whoever the fuck lived here should have been spending their money on home repairs and not pizza. Weeds had the foundation of the house in a chokehold. Even in the dim moonlight, Ron could make out the sign of rats scurrying back and forth from the old car to the front porch.

When he got to the front steps, Ron noticed that the peeling white paint covered a garish blue. The house looked old, but something about the undercoat made him think of the '70s more than anything. Maybe it wasn't as old as he thought. Maybe it was just run-the-fuck down.

The door was a dark blue with an ornate window set into the middle. A copper button for a doorbell sat to the right of the door. Ron pressed the button, setting off an annoying chime inside. That was when he realized that there weren't any lights on in the house.

"What the hell?" he whispered. "Goddamn kids."

This wouldn't be the first prank delivery he had been sent on. Anger surged through him, and he threw the pizzas at the door. It swung open with a faint creak. Ron spat over the threshold and started walking back to his car. He had just made it down the steps when he saw something moving in the trees on the other side of the road. Squinting his eyes, Ron took another tentative step forward when something large and dark broke free from the underbrush and began charging at him.

"Fuck. Fuck!" he cried as he turned and stumbled back up the steps and into the house.

Slamming the door behind himself, Ron saw that the door had a large deadbolt and slid it into place. He knew that this rotten wood wouldn't hold back whatever was coming for him. He crawled backward through the darkness as quickly as he could. The rough wood of the floor bit into his palms, but he was too scared to notice. Suddenly, the door rattled on its hinges as something slammed into it. Something clattered to the floor, causing Ron to scream.

"Down here, hurry!" a voice shouted from behind a door.

It sounded like a little kid. Maybe the dumbass who called in the prank delivery. Ron felt his fear fading. The thing from the woods must have been another kid just trying to scare him. He stood up and tried to make himself seem bigger than he really was.

"Okay, you fucking kids!" he shouted. "I'm gonna whoop your asses!"

"Mister, get down here before that thing kills you!" the child pleaded.

Then the door burst inward, and all of Ron's newfound courage melted away. He turned and threw open the door, rushing inside. His feet

went out from under him as he belatedly realized that he had rushed onto a staircase to the
basement. Tumbling down, Ron fell into deeper
darkness, landing with a crack and a shooting
pain in his elbow.

"Christ! Kid, I need help! I think my arm's
broken!"

"It's okay," the voice answered. "It doesn't
mind."

The smell of wet earth was replaced by something rotten, like the dumpster behind Qik Bite.
Ron heard a slithering sound, like something
massive was making its way toward him. He
tried to crawl back up the steps, but his arm
wouldn't work.

A dim amber light sprang from a corner,
causing Ron to cover his eyes.

"I need to see you better," the voice said, "to
get the likeness right."

When Ron uncovered his eyes, he saw the
source of the slithering sound and let out his
final scream before he was enveloped in its moist
bulk.

5

"What do you make of this?" Deputy Granger asked.

"I have no idea," Trey replied.

Sam hadn't fully woken up by the time the senior deputy knocked on her door early Saturday morning. When she opened the door and was told that Granger was actually there for Trey, Sam grumpily roused him from bed and sat glaring at the pair while sipping coffee. The bald, heavy-set deputy was holding up a photo that she couldn't make out from where she sat on the couch, which added to her grumpiness. Some shit was starting up again, and her house guest seemed to be in the thick of it already, which meant she was too.

"Can I come in?" the deputy asked, almost sheepishly.

Trey opened his mouth and then looked back at Sam.

"Yeah, whatever. It's not like I'm going back to bed," she said. "You might as well show me too, Granger, so I don't have to get everything secondhand."

The two men moved back into the living room and sat down, the deputy in the recliner and Trey on the couch beside her. Granger set a freshly printed photograph on the coffee table. It was the front seat of a car she didn't recognize, with a small porcelain doll sitting where the driver would. She leaned in and looked closer before clicking her teeth and going back to her coffee.

"This car was found outside Qik Bite this morning," Granger began. "It's registered to Ronald Lowry. Pizza delivery guy. No sign of Ron, just this weird doll that his manager swears looks just like him."

Trey picked up the photo and looked at it again, stroking the stubble on his chin. One of his many habits that she had started to ignore since he had moved in. She tried not to let her blood pressure rise while watching him. They had become good friends, but he wasn't the best roommate. Sam was hoping that in a few weeks she could convince Cynthia Anderhoff, the town's sole real estate agent, to sell the poor bastard a house so she could go back to living alone.

"I'd have to see it up close," Trey said, "but I guess I can see the resemblance. Ron was a regular at the Lodge. I'm assuming that's why you're here?"

Granger shifted uncomfortably in the recliner.

"Yes," he said. "One of the reasons. His supervisor at Qik Bite said that Ron was at the Lodge right before he came in for his last delivery. I wanted to know if he did or said anything odd? Did he seem to be in distress?"

"Not really," Trey said. Then he laughed awkwardly. "I did threaten him."

Sam covered her eyes and let out a long sigh.

Jesus Christ, he can be a dumbass, she thought.

"What do you mean?" the deputy asked.

"He was making…uh…crude remarks about my coworker, so I told him I'd 'do something stupid' if he did anything to her."

Then it was Granger who was sighing and rubbing his temples. When he looked back at the pair, his eyes met Sam's briefly. She thought that he looked scared. In over his head, she thought. They hadn't chosen a new sheriff yet—the mayoral campaign had taken precedence. That meant that the department was basically three men, and poor Granger had seniority.

"Luckily, Mr. Savage," Granger said evenly, "you have an alibi for the time of his disappearance...Look, that isn't the real reason I came here this morning. I know about your podcast. Most people who are aware of it think it's a bad idea, but not all of us. You're one of the few people who aren't willing to sit back and pretend Jackson Point is a normal town.

"And more than that, Nance trusted you somewhat, in the end. I don't know what happened to her besides the story you've told on *Backwoods Grindhouse*. I'm not sure if I believe all of it, but I believe enough. People don't just go missing and get replaced by a fucking *China Doll*. I need help on this. I need your help."

"You think this is related to Khythk'uhn?" Trey asked.

Granger shuddered and nodded. Locals still weren't accustomed to hearing the true name of the multi-dimensional goddess.

"So, are you going to deputize me?" Trey joked.

Granger looked solemn as ever.

"No, I'm not," he said in a whisper. "I have to keep your involvement a secret. If the council finds out that I've brought you in on this, then I'll be the next one to vanish."

"Fine, but we have conditions," Sam said, setting down her coffee.

"We?" the deputy asked.

"Yes, we," she replied. "You spent all of your time talking to Treyton here, and forgot that half of that shit with…Gideon wouldn't have happened without Becca and me. If you're working with him, you're working with us. I'll be looping her in as soon as you leave."

Trey leaned back with a smile, as if he had been the one to throw his weight around.

"Alright, Ms. Moore," Granger said. "What conditions?"

"First: You provide us with gear. I'm talking a CB, guns, whatever you've got access to. Second: All case files and information you obtain go through us. No secret 'open investigation' bullshit. Third: No fucking questioning what we do or have done. Once we are in this, we are all in this together, you understand?" Granger looked grim but nodded. "Fourth: You put pressure on Cynthia Anderhoff to sell Trey a house."

The deputy eyed her warily.

"Again," he said slowly, "I listened to the podcast. Mr. Savage admits to at least two murders. Why would I want to supply him with any—"

"I can always claim that it's a work of fiction!" Trey interjected. "Besides, are there any open investigations into the murder of either Arthur Tench or Clayton Abner?"

Sam smiled. He was learning. Granger swallowed and nodded again.

"Point taken. I'll bring some things over to you tonight. I can get you a radio set to a band that will just reach me. Give me a few days on the guns, I can't hide that as easily."

He stood and shook hands with them both. Sam felt the clamminess of his skin and knew that he was still nervous. If the Fifth Signet could take down the Tench family, what hope did Clarence Granger have?

Just as much as us, she thought.

"Hey, deputy," Trey called. "Why didn't y'all just go to the delivery address?"

"The damnedest thing," he said over his shoulder. "Nobody can seem to remember it, or find any trace of it written down. Almost like something won't let them remember."

As soon as the door swung shut behind Granger, Samantha swung toward Trey and stuck a finger in his chest.

"What the hell were you thinking, threatening someone at the bar?" she asked. "Are you outside your damn mind?"

"I...I beat up a kid and shot two people a few months ago, and this shocks you?" he asked dumbly.

"It's not what you did, but where you did it. You aren't supposed to be drawing attention to yourself. Hell, you promised us that no one in town would even listen to your stupid podcast, which implicates us in *everything*, Trey. I know you want to find out more, but we have to stay alive to do that!"

Trey went to the fridge and pulled out a beer. She was about to chastise him, then thought better of it. He hadn't mentioned her own day drinking once.

"Before coming to Jackson Point, I'd never so much as thrown a punch," he said after a long sip. "Then I'm here for a few days, and I'm fucking shooting people, Sam. I don't know what to say."

She purposely softened her expression and put a hand on his shoulder.

"I beat the shit out of you, too, remember? And I killed Gideon. That didn't come naturally to me either. I have a theory about that—I think being in the presence of an Elder One doesn't just warp time, but us as well. I'd bet that living here makes folks more aggressive. Not that we could ever collect enough data to confirm it."

Trey looked thoughtful for a moment.

"No, that's good," he said, his face lighting up. "I can do a little digging and base a whole episode around—"

"Are you listening to me?" she interrupted. "I'm the only Black woman in town, so I'm used to people ignoring what I say, but Jesus Christ, Treyton. We have a truce with the city council, but how long do you think that'll last with you blabbing all of their secrets into the ether?"

He sat back on the couch, deflated. Sam felt bad for a moment, and then she remembered the bodies of Kevin and Tench and all of the others. This wasn't the time to mince words.

"You want me to stop doing the show?" he asked.

"No, I want you to use your brain, and I want you to realize how exposed we all are. You aren't just putting yourself at risk, Trey. You're putting me and Becca in the crosshairs, too."

He nodded silently and nursed the beer. At first, she had hoped that he had been right and that the show would bring in some trickle of information to help them; maybe something that would allow them to leave Jackson Point, or help her in her own search for answers about her grandfather. But so far, all it had done was bring unwanted attention back on them. If Becca was too enamored with Trey to reel him in, Sam would have to do it, even if he came kicking and screaming.

They had decided to split up for the afternoon. Sam was to go and fill in Becca, while Trey went down to see the doll in person at the station. He wanted to come with Sam, but she insisted that they cover more ground right now—and she had no real idea what Ron looked like.

Bridgette's Boutique was the only real clothing store in town, and compared to anywhere in the rest of the civilized world, it left quite a bit to be desired. Still, it was a safe place for Becca to work, given their circumstances. Sam still showed up at the school each weekday, though her heart hadn't been in it since Kevin's death—or Gideon's. The school limped along without a principal or gym teacher for a few weeks before the city council moved a few things around. Now, Kenneth Fitzgerald was the principal, the pink-faced prick who used to teach music, and there were currently no athletics or gym programs.

Sam tried not to think about Gideon much, just like she tried not to think about the fact that they were living in some fourth-dimensional hell. If she hadn't figured out the reality of the Rootmother with mathematics, she figured that she would have swallowed a bullet rather than a bottle. In any case, denial was the best way to deal with some things, and her current reality fit the bill.

The outside of the store was a lavish facade, with ornate scrollwork on fake stucco pillars. Amidst the signs in the windows advertising the newest styles or whatever sales were going on, there was a political sign endorsing Melanie Thatcher for mayor. Melanie was the closest thing to a "progressive" candidate that Jackson Point could ever hope for. She wasn't from an old family, and she had a history as a larger-than-life member of the community, working first at the school, then at the credit union while volunteering at the fire department. She seemed too good to be true, which Sam figured meant that she was. Still, her opponent, Brent Doherty, was worse. Old logging money with deep connections to the town's past—and a likely member of the Fifth Signet.

Inside the store, a few mannequins sat in circular pools of light, mostly clothed in winter styles from knockoff brands. Bridgette didn't bother importing the good stuff. No one could afford it here. Sam pretended to look at the mannequins and then peruse a few clothing racks and the bargain bin until she caught Becca's eye. The bright-eyed brunette gave her a curt nod and waved her back to the fitting rooms. Usually, they didn't take such silly precautions. But with the mayoral race in full swing, it seemed that the city council was on edge, and Sam didn't want to be caught unawares.

Back at the fitting rooms, Sam slipped inside with a dress so ugly that she wouldn't even wear it to a costume party. Once the door lock clicked shut, she heard Becca from just outside the door.

"What's going on?" she asked, somewhat frightened. "Is Trey alright?"

"Yeah," Sam said. "But this couldn't wait until tonight. Some shit is going down again, and we're about to get involved. One of the deputies, Clarence Granger, came by the house to show Trey a picture. Someone went missing, and a doll that looks just like them was left in their place. He wants us to help him figure out what's going on."

"Wait," Becca said. It sounded like she was leaning against the door. "A fucking doll?"

"Yeah. Trey is heading down to the station to check it out. We're going to have access that we wouldn't normally have, and he's dropping some supplies off tonight, but we have to keep a low profile. That's why I talked to Trey about the podcast this morning, too. I think it leaves us too exposed. Thoughts?"

There was a long pause.

"Yeah, I agree."

"Good," Sam said, letting out a long breath. "I'm not saying he needs to shelve the whole thing, but he needs to be careful, especially if the council is behind this doll shit. None of us wants to end up..."

She trailed off. Trey had died and come back, Sam had been forced to kill her lover, but Becca had likely suffered the worst. Not only had her parents died in a fire, but her little sister had died over and over in front of her eyes. Then she was kidnapped and strung up naked to be used as a sacrifice. Talking about death with her wasn't a fun experience.

"No, no, we don't," Becca said after a time. "So what's next?"

"Come to my place after work, and we can get started. Hopefully, this won't be as messy as last time."

Sam wasn't about to hold her breath, though.

6

Trey pulled up in front of the police station and threw a piece of gum in his mouth. He didn't want to throw off his new partnership right off the bat by seeming drunk. After taking a moment to collect himself, he wandered inside and looked for Granger.

One of the other deputies tried to intercept him, but Trey called out loudly, "Deputy Granger! I came down to give you that official statement you asked about!"

Granger, to his credit, hid any potential surprise well. He waved Trey over and walked him back to the sheriff's desk. Tench's name still adorned the placard that sat on it, even though the desk sat empty between interviews. Trey was surprised at this, as the rumor around town was that she had actually been responsible for all of the murders last year. Though the council didn't want to go so far as to acknowledge what were likely their rumors in the first place, such as by having the department issue a warrant for her arrest, they were keen to fan the flames of public opinion. The deputy smiled genially before leaving and coming back with a cup of black coffee in a Styrofoam cup.

"What the hell are you doing here?" Granger asked through gritted teeth.

"I need to see the doll up close," Trey replied. "Remember, you hold nothing back."

"For Chrissake, I could've brought it with me tonight."

Trey slurped the coffee with exaggerated vigor.

"I know you could have, but I figured we needed to sell the idea that I'm just a witness and nothing else."

Granger grimaced for a moment before heading into one of the few doors in the small station. He returned with an evidence box and plopped it down on the table. From inside the box, the deputy produced a clear bag with a small porcelain doll inside.

He handed it over to Trey and said loudly, "Ever seen this before, Mr. Savage?"

Trey examined the doll as best he could without taking it out of the bag. It was small with white skin and a painted face like other dolls of its kind. But, in an eerie way, it did resemble Ron. The miniature clothes were the same, down to the very stains he had the night before. And its face looked molded and painted to resemble the sour little man. Pulling out his phone, Trey discreetly snapped a few pictures of the doll.

"This is uncanny," he whispered. "It's like someone turned him into this thing."

"Do you think that's possible?" the deputy asked.

"No fucking clue."

The door opened, and a voice called out from the front of the station.

"Deputy Granger!"

Both men jumped at the interruption, causing Trey to drop the doll onto the desk. He turned and saw Brent Doherty, one of the two candidates for mayor, looming in the doorway. Granger excused himself and made for the door, leaving Trey alone with the doll. He picked it up to look it over one final time when he noticed a crack running across its neck from where it had hit the table. Already, blood had begun to weep from the crack and fill the bottom of the bag.

Back in his car, Trey pulled out his phone and looked at the pictures of the Ron-doll for several minutes in silence. At first, he would have thought that the doll was just the calling card of some new occult killer. But once it started bleeding, he decided that this was something far worse. There had to be some information about this somewhere, just like the killings from last year.

I really need to come up with a name for whatever Gideon was, he thought. The distraction pulled his mind down dark paths for several minutes. It wasn't just the dying that haunted him, but the reality that something far greater than humanity lurked in the dark corners of the world, and their disposition toward humanity was not benevolent. Trey had considered himself a religious man for a long while. Now the entire idea of organized religion seemed to be a sick joke. The real higher powers weren't anything like the Sunday school stories.

Khythk'uhn.

He shuddered and tried to drive the name from his mind, but it was too late. He could almost feel her gaze focus on him. Suddenly, it was dark, and he was driving again, speeding down Main Street toward the tree where they had found Chance Bainbridge. This time, however, a naked woman stood in front of it, beckoning him with a wispy hand. Branches emerged from her crotch in a tangle, some digging into the ground like roots while others cupped her breasts. Her nipples became two black holes that swallowed all light and belched out darkness. Her eyes fell on him, and he into them; millions of stars swirled inside, a multitude of worlds inside this singular being. Then he crashed and was flying back into the tree, his head ripped from his shoulders.

Trey snapped awake. He was still sitting in his car, parked in front of the police station. It had just been another waking nightmare. His hair was plastered to his forehead from sweat. Wiping his wet hands on his pants, Trey gripped the wheel and pulled down the street.

The library was diagonal from the police station, but Trey didn't end up there until he circled the town a few times, both to calm himself and to try and picture where Ron's last delivery was. After a few loops, he began to think that it had happened down one of the side roads. A delivery down a remote forest road outside of town would be the perfect place to lure someone. Kingdom's Road, Yeller's Drive, Fincher Road, Davis Road, Wacum Road, and the nameless road that went past the Elder One's Crown. Trey drove past them all in turn, stopping to make a list in his Moleskine. He would need to do some more driving later to see if anything was amiss, though he wasn't comfortable doing that alone.

Finally, he was back at the library. The trio hadn't tried to gain access since Becca had quit. As far as they were concerned, this was currently the heart of enemy territory. In fact, Trey wasn't even sure that any books of value to them hadn't been removed—but he figured it was time to find out.

Vaulting up the steps, the podcaster pushed inside, walking past the strange paintings in the foyer and into the library proper. Never slowing his stride, Trey walked right past the front desk, purposely not looking to see if Herman was at his post. A loud throat-clearing told him that the man was, but Trey ignored him. He knew that the best esoteric and occult lore was kept in McReedy's office, but at least *Paganism & Pioneers* should have still been in the Local History section.

Though it had been months, Trey remembered his way there and angled for the stairs that led to the upper floor. As he passed the glass cube that served as McReedy's office and the Rare Book Room, he saw the old woman looking directly at him, the corners of her mouth turned downward. Considering her place in the Fifth Signet and what she had subjected Becca to, Trey flipped her off and continued on to the stairs.

When he made it to Local History, he ran his fingers along the spines, looking for the book that had given him so much information last time. It was nowhere to be found. That in itself wasn't necessarily a cause for concern, he supposed—after all, it was possible that someone had checked it out.

No, Trey thought. *No one would be interested in that book but us.*

Resolve blossomed in his chest as he descended the metal stairs, taking them two at a time. Once he was back on the ground floor, Trey beelined for the Rare Book Room. McReedy was still sitting at her desk, hands steepled as if she were waiting for him. He opened the door and sat down across from her, a wicked smile on his face.

"What are you doing here, Mr. Savage?" she asked coolly.

Before answering, Trey scanned the titles of books behind the woman. He was correct in his assumption that *Paganism & Pioneers* had been moved under her watchful eye.

"I just came to check in on you, that's all," he said glibly.

She leaned forward, smiling broadly. Her

thin, yellow teeth, coupled with her flat, dead eyes, reminded him of a barracuda. The smell of mint and baby powder wafted off her.

"Is that so?" she asked. "Well, consider me checked up on. Would you like me to check up on my former employee, Ms. White? Or what about your housemate, the Black woman?"

Trey didn't take the bait.

"Does our agreement still stand?"

"It does, for now," she whispered. "Though your little…podcast may change that. We cannot control what other enlightened ones from outside our community will do. If you keep revealing the secrets of the Fifth Signet online, you will bring down a wrath upon yourself that you cannot even fathom."

Trey pushed out his chair and stood, purposely looming over the woman as he did so.

"I look forward to it. Remember, I've died once already."

"Do you know what your name means?" she asked. "Treyton."

He paused but didn't answer.

"A town near trees. How fitting."

As he walked back outside, his legs nearly buckled from the loss of adrenaline. He needed a beer and a long moment to think—and to pretend that he hadn't just spat in the devil's eye.

7

The church bells from Forest's Hope tolled warmly. Henrietta, Willard, and their boys were dressed in their Sunday best and walking down the muddy path toward the church. It had rained hard last night, as the road still attested, though Henrietta didn't mind, as it made the air smell earthy and clean. Willard was in a fine mood today, as he often was on Sundays, being as he didn't have to work at the mill.

"How's about I take the boys out to the lake and teach 'em a little fishing this afternoon?" he asked.

"That suits me fine," she replied. "I could use a little quiet round the house."

Ahead, the steeple of the church seemed to glisten in the sunlight. Though some of the customs of Shepherd Cabot were strange to her,

Henrietta had grown fond of the little parish that brought all manner of folks together to worship. As Eliza had said to her a few nights ago, Henrietta's boys had good biblical names, after all. She couldn't imagine a world where she wasn't singing the name of Jesus on a Sunday.

Once inside, the family took their place in a middle pew. Willard pulled out the family Bible and began to read psalms quietly to the boys. Henrietta bowed her head, but looked around the room for some sign of the Winslow family. Hyrum wasn't a good man, that she was sure, but was he the god-fearing sort?

Then she saw them, sitting just behind her on the other side of the aisle. Thankfully, Hyrum didn't see her, but Eliza did. The pale woman waved at Henrietta excitedly. It seemed that she wasn't aware of the treatment Henrietta had suffered from Hyrum when last they spoke. Henrietta returned the wave and flashed a broad smile at the woman.

She seems like she needs a friend, she thought. *Lord, have mercy, she's not the only one.*

The Dollmaker finally noticed the women looking at each other, causing him to prod his wife roughly with his cane and point up at the altar. She gave Henrietta a final sheepish grin before turning forward and bowing her head.

"Welcome all!" Shepherd Cabot boomed from

the pulpit. "It is the year of our lord 1906, and what a wonderful year it has been, has it not? Our roots have been nourished this year, and our Mother smiles upon us."

Henrietta turned forward to listen to the preacher as best she could, but her mind wandered back to the Winslow family and the odd doll they referred to as Winifred.

After the service, Willard and the boys were already traipsing ahead to the house to get bait and tackle ready for their sojourn to the lake. Henrietta smiled as she watched them go, already planning for the chores that she hoped to get done while the boys were away.

"Henrietta!" a woman called.

She turned and saw Eliza and her boys coming up behind her. The woman carried a colorful blanket under one arm and a picnic basket in the other. Her husband was nowhere to be seen.

"Would you care to join the boys and me for a picnic?" she asked. "Your family is welcome too, of course!"

"Willard is taking the boys to the lake to fish, but I would be happy to come with you."

"Boys, this is Henrietta Frock," Eliza said.

Henrietta curtsied. "Henrietta, this is Alastor and Malthus."

Alastor was the older of the pair, and by the looks of it, better adjusted. Malthus was a sullen sort who wouldn't make eye contact with the woman. While Henrietta had thought them both rambunctious when she had first seen them, the younger boy now seemed anything but.

"And your daughter?" Henrietta asked.

"Ah, yes, Lamia," she said distantly. "She's with the nanny at the moment. Hyrum didn't want her to fuss through the service."

"Of course. And the man himself?"

"He'll be in meetings for the rest of the day, which is why the boys and I figured we could relax and enjoy the scenery!"

Falling in step with the trio, Henrietta followed them to a small hill overlooking the lumber mill. They spread their blanket out over the wildflowers and settled in to eat. From inside the basket, Eliza produced scones, herring, and various cheeses Henrietta had never seen before. At first, they ate in silence, but once the boys disappeared down the hill to play, Eliza's demeanor shifted.

"I'm terribly sorry about Hyrum the other night," she said. "He can be...rough around the edges. Has been ever since...well, ever since Winnie died."

Eliza must have noticed the look of confusion on Henrietta's face, for she placed her hand on the other's leg and continued.

"Winifred was my firstborn. A beautiful baby girl. She had a head of black hair right from the womb—such a gorgeous thing. We lived happily for four years until she vanished one day. They never found a trace of her…"

"Oh my Lord," Henrietta said. "Eliza, I'm so very sorry."

The woman wiped a tear with the hem of her dress.

"It still hurts, all of these years later. In any case, Hyrum, who had always been a doting father, never seemed to shed a tear. Everyone handles grief in their own way, my mother told me. So when he disappeared into his workshop after her death, I figured he was finding solace in doll-making. In a way, I was right.

"When Hyrum finally came back to me, he was carrying the very doll you returned. It was such a fantastic likeness to my Winnie that I gave the doll the same name, and we rarely travel without her. After that, Hyrum told me that he expected many more children. Though I've given him three, my health has begun to fail, and I don't know if I can survive another…"

Eliza stared off down the hill at her boys. Alastor was running and jumping and whooping like Henrietta had seen before, but Malthus simply sat and dug his fingers into the dirt. Henrietta thought that exposing him to Joshua and Ezekiel might do the boy some good.

"That's enough sadness for today, I think!" Eliza said, sounding chipper again. "What about your family? You said the boys were going fishing?"

"Yes! There is a good, deep lake near here where Willard is planning to take them. I haven't been there myself yet, but he tells me it's beautiful."

Eliza sidled closer to Henrietta, the blanket bunching awkwardly between them.

"We should go sometime, when the menfolk are busy," she said. "I'd like to get to know this place better, seeing as we're stuck here."

"Stuck here?" Henrietta asked.

"Oh...don't mind me. Hyrum just mentioned that nobody ever leaves Jackson Point, likely on account of its beauty, I would wager."

The conversation shifted again, and the women talked about their upbringings and lives before they were married. Neither had come from money, though Eliza had been fortunate to marry into it. From there, they talked about raising kids, sewing, and even the bible. It was nearly the middle of the afternoon when they decided to clean up and head back to their homes.

❦

Over the next few days, the women made a point to see each other as much as possible. Eliza started dropping by the house and sitting inside while Henrietta did her daily chores. The boys were often left back at the Winslow house with the nanny, though she brought baby Lamia with her sometimes.

Eliza was always gone by the time Willard got home, so he had yet to meet her. She wasn't allowed to be away from home when Hyrum got back from whatever it was he did during the day. It seemed that he didn't allow the nanny to be present when he was in his workshop, so it was up to Eliza to keep the children out of his hair.

The more Henrietta learned of Hyrum, the less she liked the man. It seemed that her inter-action with him was rather typical of his disposi-tion. It got to the point that she hoped never to see the man up close again. Unfortunately, that hope was dashed. Eliza had come this afternoon with her boys instead of Lamia. They were playing outside with Joshua and Ezekiel when the women heard the sound of a carriage. Eliza went paler than usual.

"It's too early for our man to be here to get us," she said. "That must mean Hyrum is here..."

The women went outside and saw that the Winslow patriarch had indeed arrived. He scowled as he looked at the Frock household, but made no acknowledgment of Henrietta herself. He was dressed in black today, and leaned on his cane more than usual. Hobbling over to the women, he addressed his wife alone.

"Someone has been in my workshop," he hissed. "The nanny claims it wasn't her."

"I couldn't imagine Suzanne would go down there, she knows—"

"Was it you?!" he shouted, spittle spraying both women.

"No, of course not, dear," Eliza said weakly. "Perhaps one of the boys got curious."

Hyrum turned and watched the four boys playing together. The silence hung between them for several agonizing minutes when the man finally whistled with two fingers, drawing Alastor and Malthus running back up to the house.

"Boys," he said in a saccharine voice, "did one of you go into my workshop?"

"No, father," they said in unison.

Then the man moved with a speed that his cane belied, grabbing Malthus by the neck and pulling the boy down so that he could examine his head. To everyone's shock, the boy's hair was filled with wriggling white strands. Hyrum pulled one out and held it between his thumb and forefinger. Henrietta stifled a gasp when she realized that it was a maggot. The boy's head was covered in writhing maggots that looked long enough to be earthworms.

"You have been in the basement!" Hyrum shouted, pushing the boy to the ground.

He lifted his cane and struck the boy on the back again and again.

"I told you never to go there! Elder Ones take you! I told you!"

Hyrum was nearly frothing at the mouth. Eliza screamed and pleaded, but the man wouldn't stop. Henrietta felt ill. She couldn't sit back and watch this, so she grabbed her rake and swung it into the man, drawing bloody lines across his face. Hyrum stopped beating Malthus and stood straight up very slowly. When he looked at Henrietta, his eyes were rimmed with blood.

"Get in the carriage," he whispered.

Eliza and the boys quietly did as they were told, without so much as looking at Henrietta.

"You've not seen the last of me, woman," he said, turning away.

"Is that so?" Willard asked.

Henrietta was overjoyed to see her husband,

covered in sweat and sawdust, walking over from across the road. What he was doing here at this time of day, she didn't know, but by God, she was thankful.

"I don't take kindly to that kind of talk about my wife," he said, squaring up with Hyrum.

"Your wife," Hyrum spat, "won't stop interfering with my family's private affairs. Do you see what she's done to my face? I could have the sheriff—"

"Your family is your business, and my family is mine. If my wife saw reason to do that to you, then you must be some kind of devil. Now get out of here before I finish what she started."

Hyrum spat on Willard but said nothing else. He climbed into the carriage, and their man, who had remained silent and stone-faced through the entire ordeal, urged the horses on and carried the Winslow family away. Henrietta fell into Willard's arms and started crying.

"I'm so glad you came," she sobbed. "How did you get out early?"

"We get the afternoon today," he said. "Something about following the will of the Root-mother. What happened? Who was that?"

Henrietta told Willard everything about the Winslow family, from the first time she saw them until now. He nodded along before telling her to keep her distance while he was working, lest something came of the man's threats. One nagging thought she kept to herself, however. Henrietta was now convinced that Hyrum had been the reason that their daughter Winifred had gone missing. She was going to be more careful, but she wasn't going to abandon that family to that cruel man.

8

"You did what?!" Becca shouted.

"I needed to see if she had moved the book," Trey said sheepishly. "That seemed like the best way to do it."

"The best way?" Sam asked. "Jesus Christ, I thought I just told you to keep a low fucking profile, Trey."

The three of them were sitting in Sam's front room, waiting for the delivery from Deputy Granger. Cold microwave dinners sat on the coffee table between them. Trey had just finished filling them in on what he had seen that afternoon at both the police station and the library. It wasn't going well.

"Look, I know you two don't like my methods, but—" Trey began.

"Methods?" Sam interrupted. "You aren't a fucking maverick cop, Trey, you are a god-damned podcaster stuck in a haunted fucking town. Get a grip!"

Becca seemed to flinch slightly as Samantha dressed him down, but she didn't jump to his defense, either; that didn't bode well. Trey was truly outnumbered. He wished Kevin were there to back him up.

Christ, he thought. *I'm wishing to be defended by a dead teenager.*

"Trey," Becca said, putting a hand on his leg. "You need to step back for a moment. We had a big win last year, and you've let it go to your head. We don't want the city council to decide to come after us again."

She looked pleadingly at Sam. The other woman nodded and then took over.

"If you want to figure out this doll thing, then you need to take a back seat," she said.

"What do you mean?" Trey asked.

"We mean that you don't do anything without running it by us first," Sam replied.

Trey rocked back against the couch. He felt Becca tighten her grip on his thigh, but his world was spinning. It wasn't like he was the leader or something; they had pretty much all been equal partners in this thing, but now it felt like he was being demoted.

"I-I don't understand," he muttered. "I mean, I thought we were in this together? The podcast… I…"

"We *are* in this together," Becca said with a squeeze. "Which is why you need to settle down. It hasn't even been twenty-four hours since Granger looped us in on this, and you're already confronting McReedy. You're putting all of us at risk, Trey."

He sighed and rubbed his temples. They were right, of course. He fucked up. He *kept* fucking up, just like he did last time.

"Okay," he whispered. "You win. What do you want me to do, mistresses?"

He gave a wink and a sly smile to both of them. Sam threw a pillow at his head. It knocked his glasses to the floor.

"You jackass," she said, laughing.

Laughter was good. Trey straightened out and put his hand over Becca's, ignoring his glasses for the time being. He needed some kind of contact to keep from spinning out of control.

"What do you want me to do about the podcast?" he asked.

"Put it on hold," Becca said. "We don't want you to stop it. You might be right, and it might help us get information from other people who are going through this, but for the moment, we need to keep our heads down. We can reevaluate after this doll shit is over."

"At least wait until we get you your own place," Sam said. "If some hooded douche-bags kick in a door to ritualistically murder you, I'd rather you be somewhere else."

They all laughed, and the tension seemed to evaporate. They were right, he had gone too far with the show. Besides, he wanted to get them more involved with it in any case. Maybe this was the way to make that happen. Something inside wouldn't let him give up *Backwoods Grindhouse* entirely. It was the one thing that allowed him to still pretend to be normal.

"Now, back to Ron," Trey said, pulling out his Moleskine and recovering his glasses. "I did some driving between the police station and the library visits today, and I think it's likely that Ron went to one of the houses out on the backroads. I think tomorrow we drive down each of them and look for any houses that seem suspicious."

"That's hundreds of houses. You know that, right?" Becca asked.

"Yeah, I know," Trey said. "I'm betting this happened at an abandoned one, though. And I think I might know it when I see it."

His mind flashed to the naked woman from his nightmare.

"How's that?" Sam asked.

"Podcaster's intuition," he joked.

Becca got up and went to the refrigerator, bringing back a round of beer for each of them. After the hisses of freshly cracked cans died down, she spoke.

"And what if your intuition fails us? What then?"

"We need access to those books," Trey replied.

"No," Sam said. "Veto. Or whatever. That'll draw too much heat, at least right now. We need to exhaust other avenues. Have you heard of the internet, mister podcaster?"

Trey took a long sip, holding up one finger for a pause.

"Fine. I'll do it the old-fashioned way," he laughed. "Still, we need those books eventually."

"Agreed," Becca said. "I'd love nothing more than to take them right out of Evelyn's bitch-ass fingers, but now that you tipped our hand..."

Trey wilted a bit as he thought back to the not-so-veiled threats from the old librarian.

"Let's start with your driving idea and go from there," Sam said. "In the meantime, Granger might turn up something that he can fill us in on."

Hours passed before the deputy arrived. When he did, he had a duffel bag in tow containing a portable radio he had already set to a frequency he would be monitoring. He also brought along flashlights, road flares, and other survivalist gear. They stood around the table as he showed off the contents of the bag.

"Are we solving a missing person's case or going camping?" Sam asked.

"You never know," the deputy said. "If shit gets bad, I want you to be able to lie low. Like I said, give me a few days and I'll have some guns for you. Just don't go shooting the next mayor, okay?"

"What *did* Doherty want with you today?" Trey asked as he zipped the duffel closed.

Granger shuffled nervously from foot to foot. It seemed that he still wasn't completely comfortable sharing everything with them. Eventually, his trepidation gave way, and he decided it was worth the risk.

"He thinks he's got the election in the bag, so he's already started throwing his weight around like he's the mayor," Deputy Granger said. "He told me he wanted a quick resolution to this case, and if I pulled it off, he would make sure I was the next sheriff."

"That's interesting," Becca said. "So does that mean he's not Fifth Signet, or is this just another smokescreen?"

"Hard to say," Granger replied. "He's from

an old family, but he doesn't seem to associate with members of the city council. The Dohertys never caused much trouble around here, even though the legend is that they lost the bidding war to the Tench family for the mill way back."

"Speaking of Tench," Sam said, somewhat hoarsely. "Any word from Nance? Anything at all?"

Granger looked down at his hands a moment before answering. When he looked up, his eyes had a wet sheen to them.

"None," he said. "I hate to say it, but I think they killed her right after you stopped them. They probably knew she wouldn't rest after they got to Arthur, so they took the most prudent option..."

The silence that followed hung over the room for a few awkward moments before Granger finally excused himself and left. It was nearly the middle of the night by now, and Trey didn't feel comfortable with Becca being out by herself.

"Will you stay the night, Becca?" he asked.

She looked at Sam first.

"I don't care," she said. "Just so long as y'all keep it down."

Trey felt his cheeks get hot, but Becca simply laughed. A few minutes later, they were in bed together, though neither was naked, and nothing went further than a tight cuddle as they drifted off to sleep.

❀

In the middle of the night, Trey awoke to find Becca staring at him. He quickly realized that she was no longer wearing her clothes. The faint light from outside outlined the curve of her breasts in silver. She never said anything, but her hands traveled down his pants and began to cup his manhood.

Moments later and he was on top of her, silently thrusting and biting his lip to keep from alerting Samantha. Becca herself seemed to be struggling equally on that front, as she had covered her face with a pillow to stifle her moans. Trey felt her back arch, and he gripped her hips, increasing the speed of his thrusts. The darkness began to pool around her nipples, causing them to look like dark lakes in the center of the moonlight.

Just as he could feel himself about to climax, Becca removed the pillow and locked eyes with him. Inside her eyes, he could see millions of stars again. Trey tried to pull away from her, but he could feel something rough and solid holding him in place. Then a branch erupted from between her legs and stabbed into him, shredding his body from the waist down.

Trey collapsed onto the floor in a puddle of blood, twitching as the last of his life ebbed away. Becca stood over him, her body fully that of Khythk'uhn now. He felt himself pulled into the black holes on her breasts, fading with the light that was sucked into them.

The next morning, Trey already knew what he would find. Both he and Becca were covered in blood beneath the sheets. She had also had a similar dream, though Trey had resembled the Gideon-monster in hers. Both of them sat on the floor in opposite corners of the room in silence until they heard Sam stirring in the next room.

"We better go out together so she doesn't think I killed you or something," Trey said with a forced smile.

Becca snorted.

"One of these times we just need to get this over with and fuck," she said. "Can't be worse than the dreams…"

Then she looked down at herself again, and Trey wasn't sure that she actually believed that. They waited a few more minutes until they heard the trickle of the coffee pot. Trey checked his phone and saw that it was Sunday, as it should be. That meant all three of them had the day off to try and figure some shit out. That was good, at least. He opened the door and walked out first, with Becca close behind. When Sam saw them walk into the kitchen, she dropped her coffee onto the floor.

"Bad dream," they both said.

9

The trio started their day at Eaton's General Store after Becca and Trey cleaned themselves up. Sam hadn't asked any further questions, other than whether or not her guest bed was ruined. After Gideon had kidnapped Becca last year, none of them truly felt comfortable shopping alone. While Sam and Trey looked for donuts and iced coffees, Becca chatted with Carrie, her friend who often worked the register here.

"He hasn't been the same since the sheriff killed the mayor," Carrie said in a whisper. They had been talking about Eaton Marsh, the grocery store owner and cult member.

"What do you mean?" Becca asked coyly. Carrie had always been a gossip.

"Well, for starters, he hasn't been as…*handsy* lately."

"That's good!"

"Yeah, for sure. But he's also been quite a bit meaner. He's working less, and when he does show up, he looks…older. I don't know how else to describe it. It's like he's pushing eighty all of a sudden."

That was something to make note of, Becca thought.

Maybe Granger was right, and this was Fifth Signet. If Eaton was acting stranger than usual, that meant they were up to something. It had to be the doll, right?

"Anything else weird happen lately?" Becca asked.

"Not that I can think of," Carrie said. "Why're you so curious? You normally couldn't care less about what goes on 'round here."

"You know how it is," Becca said, casting a longing glance at Trey.

"Ah. Changing for a man. Figures."

Becca blushed just as Trey and Sam walked up with breakfast and drinks. Carrie made pleasant small talk while they checked out, but her eyes kept flitting from Becca to Trey. Thankfully, she didn't say anything untoward.

They climbed back into Sam's car, Becca in front and Trey in the back. He could be a gentleman when he had his brain turned on, which seemed to be the case today. Becca took a bite of a maple bar and slurped down the coffee. She always used to share donuts with Jenni. Her sister's screams filled her ears and soured her appetite.

"Which road first?" Sam asked.

"Kingdom's Road," Trey replied. "Doesn't it split off to Death Street or something?"

"Murder Creek," Becca said. "Believe it or not, there was a murder there, once."

"You don't say?" Trey laughed.

She liked the sound of his laugh. Too bad she didn't like the way he treated her in her dreams.

Eaton's was only a few blocks away from Kingdom's Road. Everyone else had finished their donuts before Sam turned to the outer reaches of Jackson Point. Becca had grown up on one of the town's outer roads. Once her home had burned down, she had moved into town to finish out High School living with friends. Since then, she hadn't left the town proper. Doing so today didn't particularly excite her.

"We can look at homes for sale, too!" Sam said with fake enthusiasm.

Becca knew Sam was ready to have her space

back. Trey was welcome to move in with her, but there wasn't much space in her trailer for another person unless he slept with her, and after last night…

"I get it," Trey said, leaning forward so he was between the two women. "Once we get through this, I'll start looking for something."

"No, it's fine, really," Sam said sarcastically. "Who doesn't like bloody guest sheets and the fear of a multi-dimensional being showing up in their house?"

"Hey, you're the one who shot her 'son', remember?" Trey said with a smirk. "I don't think that earned you any favors from the ol' Rootmother."

The car fell into an awkward silence as the trees closed in around them. The side roads around town were lined with homes set back into the trees. It would take the majority of the day to catalog them all, and even then, would they really know the place when they saw it?

In the back, Trey played with the CB radio. So far, they hadn't heard anything from Deputy Granger, which Becca figured was a good sign. Maybe Ron was going to be a freak thing? A one-off? She sighed as she remembered what Carrie had told her.

"Something is going on with the council members," she said. "Carrie says Eaton hasn't been himself. And he looks twenty years older. This has to be connected to Ron, yeah?"

Trey played with the buttons even as he answered.

"That's...worth following up on. Maybe they turned Ron into the doll? Some kind of essence transfer? Or magic that drains their life force to use? McReedy looked the same as she did before...maybe they'll be taking turns with the spell."

"What the hell are you talking about?" Sam asked. "Magic? Essence transfers? We don't know anything about what the Fifth Signet can do besides whatever happened to Gideon. Let's not jump to some Dungeons and Dragons nonsense."

"Fair enough," Trey sighed. "Just throwing out ideas."

They passed several houses without incident. Nothing stuck out to any of them, and none of the homes looked abandoned. After a while, they turned off on Murder Creek and kept going. These homes were much different than the previous batch. Most of them were set closer to the road than the homes on Kingdom's. Of those, only a handful seemed to be inhabited.

"Check that one out," Trey said, pointing at a single-level home with a sagging porch and a missing door. There were ruts from tires in front of the house that looked like they could have been fresh.

Sam swung into the driveway and killed the engine. Other than the tire tracks, this house didn't look like anyone had so much as set foot on the property in a decade. What Trey hoped they would find, she wasn't sure. He wrote down the address in his notebook and hopped out. The two women looked at each other and sighed before following him.

The porch groaned under their weight, but surprisingly held. Trey pushed in the door and powered on his flashlight. The beam cut through the darkness in a gray, dust-filled line. The inside of the house smelled like mold and animal shit. Becca covered her nose as she followed close behind Trey.

"So, uh, podcaster intuition?" she asked.

"Kinda," Trey said.

They passed through the front room and into what had once been the kitchen. The light in this room was better, as the windows here weren't boarded up, but that was the only thing this room had going for it. The refrigerator had a collection of flies buzzing around its open door. The smell in here was even worse. In the back of the kitchen, a small table was flipped on its side. The trio walked around the table and saw a pile of old blankets formed into a makeshift bed. Trey knelt down and dug through them.

"It almost looks like someone has been sleeping here recently," he said.

"That doesn't make any sense," Sam said.

"Why not?" Trey asked as he stood.

"We don't have homeless people here," Becca said solemnly. "They...don't last long."

"Ah." Trey pushed open another door and started to gag. "Well, the bathroom smells like it's been used."

He quickly pulled the door closed. Just then, they heard a banging sound from the front.

"Who's in there?" a man called.

Sam slid her pistol out of her pocket and pulled the hammer back. She waved the two of them behind her and crept back to the door that led back to the front room.

"You left your car out front!" the man shouted. "It doesn't take a genius to know someone is inside."

"Malcolm?" Trey asked loudly. It seemed he recognized the voice.

The podcaster stepped around Samantha, who hissed in distaste. He didn't seem to notice.

"That you, white boy?" Malcolm called back.

When Trey didn't cry out in pain or surprise, the two women followed him back into the darkness of the front room. Trey was shining the flashlight beam low enough not to blind the man standing in the doorway. He looked vaguely familiar to Becca, but she didn't know him well. She flushed at that.

He's probably the only native guy in town, she thought. *How do I not know his name?*

"What are you doing here?" Trey asked.

Beside her, Becca could feel Sam was still holding her gun leveled at the newcomer discreetly.

"I could ask you the same thing," the man replied.

"Do...do you live here?" Trey asked.

"What gave it away?" Malcolm asked. "The tepee?"

Sam laughed, though she didn't lower the gun.

"You make a good first impression on everyone, don't you?" she asked.

"Can we go outside where it doesn't smell like shit and piss, please?" Malcolm asked.

They followed the man outside. He stepped off the porch and eyed it warily when it groaned under the weight of the trio.

"You can put the piece away, miss," he said to Sam. "Even if you are trespassing, I'm not here to hurt anyone."

Sam slid the revolver back into her pocket, but didn't remove her hand.

"It…uh…looked abandoned," Trey said.

"It is," Malcolm replied. "That doesn't mean it's yours to just go up and claim, Columbus. Nobody's lived here for years, not since the owner killed his wife and then himself. Sad shit. Anyway, I live a house over and keep an eye on it, to make sure nobody strange starts messing around in there."

"It looked like someone had been sleeping in the kitchen," Becca said, trying to cover for Trey's obvious discomfort.

"Nope. Haven't seen anyone," Malcolm said. He spit onto the overgrown yard. "Best it stays that way. This house isn't a place for the living anymore."

"What about the tracks?" Sam asked.

"Some dumb kids looking for a good place to smoke dope," Malcolm answered. "I scared them off, of course. Now, you gonna make me stand out here all day, or are we done?"

"No, uh…we're going," Trey said.

"Good deal. You ladies have a nice day. You, too, white boy," he said with a smirk.

Malcolm turned and walked back down the road and vanished into the trees dividing the two properties. Becca let out a breath she didn't know she was holding in.

"Friend of yours?" she asked.

"I met him at the Lodge the night Ron disappeared," Trey answered. "I don't think that's a coincidence."

"Probably not," Sam said, walking back to the car. "But I don't think this is our house, anyway. Look at the tracks again. Did Ron do pizza deliveries in a big-ass truck?"

Trey bent down to examine the muddy ruts in front of the house.

"Well, I'll be damned," he said.

"Come on, detective," Sam said playfully. "We've got a lot of ground to cover still."

They spent the rest of the day driving up and down the backgrounds, writing down the address of every abandoned house that they passed. Trey's "podcaster intuition" never flared up again, and none of them were particularly eager to jump out and explore another empty house, especially as the sun started to get lower in the sky.

Finally, they hit the part of Fifth Street where it split into Wacum and Davis. Becca had been dreading this moment all day. She had no desire to drive back by the ruins of her family home. If the other two thought about that, they gave no sign. She considered asking Sam to drop her back off at home, but didn't want to embarrass herself.

"Which one?" Sam asked.

"Davis first," Trey said. "Unless you think otherwise? Becca?"

She shook her head. Words were going to be difficult for the next little bit. Outside her window, Becca saw Jenni running out of the trees, covered in flames. Her clothes were melting to her skin, and her face was a mask of pain.

"Becca?" Trey asked. "You okay?"

"Yeah," she croaked. "My...my parents lived on Davis."

"Fuck," Sam whispered. "Let's call it a day."

"No, it's fine," Becca lied.

"Trey," Granger said over the radio. "Trey, you there? Over."

Excitedly, Trey grabbed the microphone and clicked the button.

"Yeah, deputy, I'm here," he said. "Uh...over."

"I found another doll," Granger said. "Get over here to Manifest Destiny before I call it in."

Trey looked at Sam and Becca. Wordlessly, Sam swung the car and headed back to the cemetery. Becca felt relieved, and then guilty. She didn't have to face her trauma tonight, but only because someone else was likely dead.

10

They parked next to Granger's squad car and jumped out, each with a flashlight in hand. The deputy stood toward the back of the cemetery by himself. The sun had just started setting behind the trees, causing the shadows of the headstones to stretch away from them in long, inky lines. A cool breeze blew off the mountain, causing Trey to shiver.

The trio crunched through the dead grass and past the graves until they were standing in front of Granger. On the ground, lying against a tombstone, was another porcelain doll. This one looked like a woman. It had bright yellow hair and a pink dress. Trey didn't recognize who the doll was supposed to be right off, but Sam covered her mouth in shock.

"That looks just like Mary Simmons!" she exclaimed.

"That's who I think it is," Granger said solemnly. He looked paler than usual, and a sheen of sweat on his forehead caught the last broken rays of the sun.

"Who's that?" Trey asked.

"A fourth-grade girl," Granger replied. "Her mother reported her missing this afternoon. Apparently, she never came home after school. They said she had been talking about a new friend lately, but her parents don't know the kid's name."

Sam knelt and gingerly picked up the doll. She cradled it to her chest while quietly sobbing. Trey was about to put his hand on her back, but Becca beat him to it. He tried to force down the nausea as he looked back at the deputy.

"How'd you find the doll?" he asked.

"The grave digger—Alistair, called it in. He didn't know what to make of it, but he'd heard something about what happened to Ron, so he figured I'd wanna see it. Thankfully, I was the one who got the call, so nobody else knows yet."

"Jesus Christ," Trey whispered, leaning in. "A kid, again? What the fuck is with you people?!"

Deputy Granger looked away, staring off into the trees.

"I don't want this job anymore," he said distantly. "It's too goddamned much. I can't deal with the kids…I can't."

Trey clenched his fist as he watched his two friends crying together over what amounted to the corpse of a nine-year-old girl. He wanted nothing more than to take Sam's gun and drive from house to house, killing everyone he knew was in the cult. It wasn't just an idle fantasy, but a monstrous urge that he was struggling to contain.

"When can you get us the guns?" he said through clenched teeth.

The deputy looked back in horror, as if he had read Trey's mind.

"You can't be thinking of that right now…" he trailed off.

"I am!" Trey barked, his voice echoing off the graves. "Somebody has to stop this! Fuck, I should have taken them all out last year."

Becca reached back and gently grabbed him by the leg.

"Trey," she said softly.

"How many more kids have to die, you fucking coward?" Trey asked. "Give me your fucking gun and the keys to your fucking car, and I'll end this *tonight*."

"Trey!" Becca said louder.

He unclenched his fist and looked down at her. Becca's eyes were rimmed with tears, but there was a hardness there too. His anger subsided to a manageable level, and he took a few deep breaths before looking back at the deputy.

"I'm sorry," he said. "That wasn't fair. I...I'm not handling this very well."

Granger cleared his throat and nodded.

"Did you find anything today?" the deputy asked.

"Maybe," Trey said. "We checked on some abandoned houses on the outskirts of town. One of them looked like somebody had been living in it, though I don't know if it's connected to this. Do you know a guy by the name of Malcolm... Bryant, I think it was?"

"Indian guy?" Granger asked. Trey flinched but didn't correct him. "Yeah, I know who he is. He's never had any run-ins with us, if that's what you're asking. Seems nice enough. I think Nance knew him from somewhere. They'd get each other coffee sometimes. Why?"

"He talked to me at the bar the night Ron disappeared," Trey said. "I didn't think anything of it until he also found us in that abandoned house where someone was staying. Says he's a neighbor and nobody's been there. He's hiding something, I just don't know what."

"I'll look into it," Granger said. "I'll try and have the other stuff you need dropped off by tomorrow. But I don't need you going on a killing spree. We don't know if that'll even stop this."

Trey swallowed and gave a curt nod.

"Tomorrow I'll try and figure out who this new friend of Mary's is…was," Granger said.

"Look!" Becca hissed.

Both men's heads snapped up to see the silhouette of a child at the back of the cemetery. From this distance, it was hard to tell if it was a boy or a girl, but they seemed to be watching the group. Sam and Becca slowly stood, never taking their eyes off the kid. Granger slowly raised a hand like he was at a traffic stop.

"Hey there!" he called out in a sickly-sweet voice. "I'm Deputy Granger! Can I talk to you for a moment? Maybe help you get back to your parents?"

The kid bolted into the trees behind Manifest Destiny.

"Don't let them get away!" Trey shouted, flipping on his flashlight and charging after them.

Maybe this was Mary's new friend. Maybe that was Mary herself, and they weren't too late. He tripped over a smaller headstone, cracking his shin and landing on his face. Blood trickled down his nose from where his glasses cut him, but they were thankfully still in one piece. Becca came up beside him, but he waved her on.

"Just keep going," he wheezed. "We can't lose the kid."

After a moment of catching his breath, Trey was back on his feet and running into the trees.

It was closer to full darkness than twilight inside the trees. Already, a thin mist had risen from the floor of pine needles and old leaves that hadn't decayed during the winter snows. Trey had lost sight of both the child and his friends. All he could see in any direction were trees.

"Fuck this," he muttered.

The woods around Jackson Point were possibly the last place he wanted to be alone. He knew that more than wild animals stalked these trees. That was a given. Whether or not they were hunting tonight was another question entirely.

"Kid!" a voice shouted from Trey's left. "It's not safe out here! Where are you?"

It sounded like Becca, but with the natural barrier of the trees, Trey wasn't sure. He flashed his light around, scanning the underbrush for any signs of the kid before moving on. He wasn't running now—his little fall had made that choice seem unwise. Instead, he picked his way forward methodically, attempting to keep a straight line so that he wouldn't end up turned around and lost.

While he kept searching, Trey racked his brain, trying to connect the few pieces of information that they had so far. What connected the pizza guy and this little girl? The killings last year had been a ritual to awaken Khythk'uhn. Was this the same thing, or something else?

Something else, Trey thought. It's the dolls. *The dolls are the key. What the fuck is with the dolls?*

He made a mental note to do some research into occultism and dolls in the morning. Maybe this was some kind of voodoo thing? Whatever the case, if they didn't catch this kid, they needed to know what the dolls meant.

A branch snapped ahead of him. Trey raised his light but didn't see anything.

"Hello?" he called. "Kid?"

There was no answer. Another branch snapped, this time, behind him. Trey turned to see a glimpse of the kids running behind the trees. He thought for a moment that the kid had short black hair, but it was hard to tell for sure. What Trey was sure of was that the kid had the same style as an old man. It looked like they were wearing cotton trousers and an old, stuffy-looking shirt. Almost like the kid was cosplaying as a pioneer.

"Hey!" Trey shouted, running in the direction the kid disappeared in.

Moments later and the kid was nowhere to be seen, and Trey was completely turned around. The ache in his shin grew worse as the damp from the mist started to set in. Trey wasn't sure why, but he knew that he needed to find this kid and get out of the forest quickly, or he wasn't getting out at all.

"The kid is over here!" he shouted, hoping to draw the others.

"Trey!" either Becca or Sam called, their voices distant.

"Sam! Becca! Granger!" Trey shouted again. "I just saw the kid!"

Then Trey heard multiple gunshots and Granger screaming in pain. Forgetting everything but his need to get back out of the woods, Trey started running straight ahead, praying that it was the right direction.

"Trey!" a voice called, even more distant this time.

The mist had gotten so thick now that it was a full-on fog. Trey could barely see past the nearest few trees. Those beyond the wall of gray looked like crooked, dead fingers. Something was terribly wrong. They had fallen into a trap.

Another scream, this time from one of the women, followed by another hollow gunshot.

Trey ran as fast as he could, ignoring the pain in his leg. He had to get out of the trees. Then he could figure out what to do. Then he could find Sam and Becca or call for help. He just had to get out. The ground beneath his feet started to buckle upward, as if something massive was trying to burst out to the surface.

A woman stepped out in front of him from behind one of the trees. Trey raised his flashlight, but it was actually Sam's revolver. He squeezed the trigger, and the woman's head snapped back with a cracking sound. He fired again, causing a hole to tear through her breasts. Shooting her had been easy. Just like with Tench and Abner.

The woman's head snapped back into place. She reached for him, her star-filled eyes drawing him in. Branches from the trees wrapped around Trey and pulled him toward the woman. When he was close, she grabbed his head and tore it from his shoulders, pressing it into the bloody hole in her breast. Trey opened his mouth and suckled at her blood.

Trey opened his eyes to see the moon hanging overhead. He was lying on the ground of Manifest Destiny, where he had tripped. Had he hit his head? Had he even made it into the forest? His head ached, that was for sure, and something was tickling his scalp. Sitting up, Trey scanned the area for the others. There was no sign of them. He brushed his hands through his hair, shaking a bunch of small white strands out. He realized that they were maggots as soon as they hit the ground. Trey scampered backward, trying to stand without screaming.

Suddenly, Becca was running out of the trees, pulling Sam along with her. Both women were bleeding from their heads and chests.

"Get to the car!" Becca shouted at Trey.

Dumbfounded, he ran back to Sam's car and clambered into the back seat. A few moments later, the women were in and the car was speeding off, throwing gravel in its wake.

"What happened?" Trey asked, staring back at the cemetery. "Where's Granger?"

"He's dead," Sam said. "It killed him."

11

Even with the warnings from both of their husbands, Henrietta and Eliza continued to meet in secret while Hyrum was busy in his workshop or at city council meetings. While she didn't fear Willard's reaction, Henrietta also made sure to keep the visits a secret from him as well, lest he worry unnecessarily.

Mostly, the two women chatted about everything and nothing while sewing or doing the Frock family laundry. Eliza said that she was happy to help with Henrietta's domestic duties—she wasn't able to do them at her own home, even though she always wanted to. Today, the pair worked on adding patches to a new quilt that was intended for baby Lamia. It was a great big thing, with patches added in various shades of blue and green. Eliza wanted it to remind them of the sea, a sight she didn't expect her family to ever see again.

Eliza was adding a sky-blue square when she pricked her finger with her needle.

"Elder Ones!" she hissed, sucking on her finger.

"What did you say, dear?" Henrietta asked. She had heard Hyrum use the same words, and the implication that the family wasn't truly Christian bothered her nearly as much as Hyrum's violence.

"Oh, that..." Eliza trailed off. "I don't know exactly what it means. Hyrum says it often. I know it sounds blasphemous on the surface, but I don't think he means it that way. He's baptized, you see. All of us are. It's just a strange saying he picked up somewhere during his travels."

Henrietta wasn't entirely convinced, but she decided to seize the chance to find out more about the man instead. The woman had been unwilling to discuss the man since his last encounter with the Frock family.

"Travels?" she asked. "Does he travel often? Abroad?"

"Oh...uhm..."

"It's alright, dear, you know you're safe with me."

"Of course. Yes, Hyrum used to travel frequently, especially after Winnie passed," Eliza said. She looked out the window at the four boys playing in the street. "All kinds of exotic places. Burma, the British Raj, Ireland, and even Africa. He traveled to share his dolls and to learn new techniques. Here at home, he's been everywhere in the Union you can think of. Oh, how I wish he had taken me with him just once!"

Henrietta tried to hide a scowl. She had nothing against the man traveling the world, but it seemed that he did so at the neglect of his family. And perhaps this was how he had picked up such heathen phrases.

"Those sound like quite the adventures Hyrum has been on. Why, I've not been many places myself besides Boston and here. I'd like to see more of the country myself, though I don't know if I've the stomach to travel the globe!"

The women laughed, and the conversation moved on to other subjects, though Henrietta kept trying to steer it back to Hyrum and his temper. Eventually, the boys came inside, drenched as it began to rain. Joshua was first, and he refused to let the others in without using the password: "towering pine". The woman made them strip bare and hang their clothes in front of the fire. The four sat in the corner of the room under four blankets, shivering and laughing—all except Malthus, who stared into the corner, refusing the comfort of the blanket.

Eliza was clearly uncomfortable at the boy's aberrant behavior; she had started to pick at her fingers nervously whenever she looked his way. When her eyes would come back to Henrietta, she would force a fake smile and attempt to resume discussing Lamia, refusing to sleep most nights.

Outside, the wind began to howl, blowing the shutters open and shut on the windows, casting a torrent of rain inside the small house. Henrietta scrambled to secure them, getting her dress wet in the process. She sighed when she finished and plopped back into her chair. The quilt was done, a fine display of oceanic coloring...other than the small red splotches on Eliza's end. It seemed that the woman had pricked herself more than once.

"Eliza, dear," Henrietta whispered, leaning in close. "Are you sure you're alright? Your hands..."

Eliza looked down at the self-inflicted scratches and small scabs from the needle. Though she was smiling when she looked up, her eyes glistened with tears.

"I need to be more careful," she whispered. "Carelessness can lead to all kinds of troubles." She looked at the boys. "Once this rain subsides, we must be going. I'll see if one of the neighbors can take us back in a wagon or something. No need to wait for our driver..."

Henrietta grabbed Eliza by the wrist.

"Eliza, what is Hyrum doing to you and the boys? Does he hurt you often?"

"No!" Eliza said, a little too loudly. The boys looked for only a moment before they returned to their own discussions. "He doesn't hurt us. Yes, he demands discipline from the boys and me, but he isn't a cruel man. He was just agitated the other day..."

"You can tell me the truth, Eliza," Henrietta continued. "Hyrum is the reason Malthus is so quiet, isn't he? I've heard of children who hide inside themselves to escape a violent father."

"N-no," Eliza stuttered. "He's just a sensitive boy, truly. Don't fret about it."

Then she pulled back and went back to staring at the boys. Henrietta decided that she wouldn't let that be the end of it.

"You can stay with us. I've already talked with Willard," she lied. "I don't think Malthus is safe."

"You don't know what he is," Eliza whispered without looking back. "You don't know what he has done. What he is capable of doing."

"Did he kill Winifred?" Henrietta asked.

Eliza struck her across the face. The blow wasn't hard, but it was so unexpected that Henrietta rocked back in her chair. The boys stopped talking and stared at their mothers in silence—even Malthus.

"Boys, get dressed," Eliza hissed. "We are leaving."

Her mouth was set in a hard line, but tears flowed freely now. Henrietta was still in shock from being struck. No words came to her, no matter how hard she tried to find them. Alastor and Malthus got dressed in the awkward silence before being ushered out the door by thier mother. Once they were in the pouring rain, the women locked eyes with Henrietta one final time.

"Stay away from my family," she said. "Don't ever speak to me again."

Though her face was a snarl, her voice lacked any semblance of emotion. Eliza slammed the door and disappeared into the storm. Henrietta still sat dumbstruck.

It was dark when Henrietta finally started to worry. The boys had gone out playing after the storm moved on, more out of a need to be away from their silent mother than anything. But now it was late, and neither had returned.

"Where are the boys?" Willard asked as he shuffled inside.

"I-I don't know," Henrietta mumbled. "They were playing outside after the storm, but...but they should have been home by now."

Willard tensed, his huge shoulders flexing beneath his dirty shirt. Then he enveloped his wife in a hug and kissed her hair. She melted into him, some of her anxiety flaking away.

"They'll be back any moment, I'm sure," he said. "They're good boys. Better than I was." He took her face in his hands. "Good lord help me, I'd vanish in the woods for days at their age. My mother had practically bought a coffin before I was even half-grown."

Henrietta laughed. Willard always said the right thing. That was how he had successfully courted her all those years ago. His warmth changed her mood and helped her drive the afternoon confrontation from her mind. There would be time to worry about that tomorrow.

Willard changed into his night clothes and sat by the fire, filling a bowl of stew for the four of them. Though he pretended not to be worried, Henrietta noticed that he never took a bite, even long after he handed her a bowl.

The night wore on, and the boys never returned.

"I'm going to find them," Willard announced, setting his cold dinner aside. Before she could offer to join him, he said, "Stay here in case they return."

Her husband threw a coat over his night-clothes and grabbed a lantern. Then he, too, disappeared into the darkness of Jackson Point.

The following morning, they still had seen no sign of either Joshua or Ezekiel. Henrietta was so worried that she had alternated between lying down and vomiting for the entire night. Willard had returned just before sunup, bleary-eyed and covered in grime.

"The rains made all the woods a mud hole," he said, stripping. "I'm changing into better clothes and then grabbing some men from the mill. We won't start work until the boys are home safe."

Henrietta nodded silently. There was nothing for her to say. She also changed, this time into a fresh dress that she could pin more easily so that she could traipse through the woods with her husband. He knew better than to dissuade her this time. When they both were ready, the pair walked out into the early morning twilight.

Within the hour, they had a band of men following them to the edge of town. Willard had checked the woods on the eastern side the night before, so now they would focus on the west before doubling back. Henrietta felt a pang of fear in her belly when she counted the number of searchers among them. Men from the mill had joined without question, but no loggers or others who might know the terrain of the forest better had been willing.

She has them now, Henrietta thought. They were the words of the second logger her husband had asked for help. Willard had nearly punched the man before one of his friends held him back. *The Rootmother. The Bitch of the Bark.* The heathen superstitions of the natives of Jackson Point. She shuddered and tried to ignore the thoughts of her boys strapped to some Satanic altar. No—they were good Christian boys, the Lord would protect his own.

Once the group reached the wall of trees, they split into four equally-sized groups, each taking a slice of the forest beyond. At least one man in each troupe carried a gun to fire into the air if they found the boys. Willard was still attempting to project calm, but Henrietta could see the fear in his eyes as he glanced at each fir and pine. He had never looked so fearful in all the years she had known him. That made the bile rise back in her throat, but she was able to keep it down. If he saw her retching in the bushes, he would likely send her home.

Hours passed, and they didn't find anything. The demeanor of the search party began to grow sour. Some of the men grumbled about turning around, but Willard was able to silence them with a glare. They were spread out in pairs just out of reach of one another to ensure that every inch of the forest was covered. Henrietta had started to cry openly as hope fled her body.

Then she heard it.

A single retort of a pistol off to the distant right. Willard grabbed her by the hand, and the pair started running in the direction of the sound. Ahead, they could hear shouts, but she couldn't tell if they were in exultation or distress.

Through the trees, Henrietta saw a crowd forming as men from one of the other parties started to clump together in a rough circle. Someone inside was shouting, "Are you alright, boy?"

Willard shoved through the crowd, pulling his wife with him. In the center, Joshua was lying in the mud, unmoving. Henrietta dropped to her knees and pulled him close. His breaths were shallow, but by God, he was still breathing.

"He's alive!" she shouted. "Joshua, wake up! Where is your brother?"

The boy's eyelids fluttered, but he didn't wake.

"Over here! Willard, come see this!" a man shouted.

Her husband vanished from sight for a few moments. Henrietta wiped the muck from her son's face with her dress. His skin was so cold. The crowd started to move over to see what Willard was looking at. Their voices were mostly mumbles, though she thought she heard a man take the Lord's name in vain.

Willard trudged back, his face downcast.

"What?" she asked. "What is it? Is it Ezekiel? Did something happen to him?"

Willard held out a small porcelain doll that looked just like their son. Henrietta knew that the boy was dead. She let out a wail and clutched her surviving son to her breast.

"We will keep looking," Willard whispered. "I don't know what to make of this doll, and the ground is broken and covered in some kind of sap or something...but there is no sign of Ezekiel. He must be nearby."

Henrietta nodded and said nothing. She knew that he was gone just as sure as she knew who had done it. Her thoughts became scattered, and her head felt like it was full of cotton. Just before her vision blacked out, she noticed that her son's hair was full of white strands.

Maggots.

12

It looked as if the entire town had gathered to watch the couple load their car. Trey, Becca, and Sam stood silently off to the side as Jillian and Michael Simmons carried a few small suitcases out of their home.

It was Monday, the day after their daughter had gone missing, the day after a doll in her likeness had been found in the cemetery, the day after Deputy Granger had been gutted in the woods. Becca and Sam had both called in sick to work. Neither of them could go on like things were normal today. Trey was considering doing the same thing before his shift started, though he hadn't shaken the feeling that he needed to be at the Lodge tonight.

Sam pushed ahead, pulling Trey and Becca with her like they were small children.

"Jillian," she said softly. "You can't be serious about this. We don't know what happened to Mary. You can't go."

The woman dropped her bag to the ground and stared the teacher down. Trey felt himself wither inside, even though he was only on the periphery of the woman's gaze.

"She's gone," Jillian said, her voice cracking. "She's nourishing the roots, now. We can't stay here another night. Not without our little girl."

Sam tensed. If Trey had to pick one singular trait that defined Samantha Moore, it would be that she wanted to protect children, especially those at her school, above all else.

"You can't go," Sam said. "You know what happens to people who leave."

"Nothing worse than people who stay," Michael quipped as he loaded the last bag and slammed the door shut.

"How long can we keep sacrificing our children?!" Jillian shouted to the crowd. "How long can we keep feeding our babies to *her*? And for what? Because that's what we've always done?"

"Mrs. Simmons," a deep voice said.

The trio turned to see Brent Doherty wading through the crowd. He was a large man, less well-built than Arthur Tench had been, but just as imposing. His mustache was nicely groomed, and his brown hair was slicked back like he was an extra in *Goodfellas*. He was even wearing the blue suit to match. "I promise you that the sheriff's department and I will be working closely together in the coming months to get to the bottom of this. Deputy Granger..."

Trey stopped paying attention to the mayoral hopeful as his mind wandered back to the previous night and what Becca and Sam had seen happen to Granger. If he hadn't woken up in his bed today, he wasn't coming back.

"Brent, that's enough," a woman Trey didn't immediately recognize said as she walked up.

"Melanie," Brent said harshly.

Melanie was an older woman, but not frail. Even with her mostly gray hair, she looked as if she could take the man in a fight. In sharp contrast to the larger man, she was wearing a tracksuit.

"This isn't the time for some bullshit stump speech," Melanie said. "Leave that for the debate. Let these good people go and grieve in peace."

Ah, Trey thought. *That's where I've seen her before; she's the other person running for mayor.*

Trey's assessment of the woman rose in that moment as she forcefully moved her opponent away from the Simmons family. The crowd started to follow them, more interested in the impromptu mayoral debate than in the grieving parents running away from Jackson Point.

Then it was Cynthia Anderhoff who walked up and gave them each a hug. She grimaced at Trey, but thankfully ignored him otherwise.

"Are you sure about this?" she asked. "You don't want me to sell the house?"

Jillian looked back at her home one last time before handing the keys to Cynthia.

"No, we don't," she replied. "If we make it somewhere, we don't even want the money from this place. Burn the fucking thing for all I care."

Then the couple climbed into their car and drove through the gap in the crowd, swinging widely onto Main Street and out toward Jackson Highway and Cascade Locks beyond. Trey knew the stories. Nobody could leave Jackson Point permanently. Anyone who tried was either trapped physically—like he was, or mentally—meaning suicide was soon to follow once they were outside of the town's borders for more than a day or two. He hoped for their sake that it was the former, and they'd end up driving back into town without any idea that they had gotten turned around.

"There's a house available," Trey said, trying to lighten the mood.

Sam and Becca both glared at him, turning back and walking down the block. Trey sighed and quickly followed after them.

"Not the right time," he mumbled.

Neither woman said a word back.

The rest of the day was spent in relative silence. Trey focused his research online while Sam and Becca went out for coffee and brunch without him. At first, his searches provided few results. Simply typing "Khythk'uhn" into various search pages brought him exactly zero results, which shouldn't have been possible. *Backwoods Grindhouse*, at the very least, should have popped for the name. He had used the name in more than one episode description in the hope that it would bring people to the show who were doing exactly what he was doing now.

By noon, while he was on his third beer and starting to eye the clock frequently in the fear that he would be late to work, Trey stumbled across *something*.

He was scrolling through the occult section on a website filled mostly with whining incels and racism masquerading as free speech when he found a reference to the Elder Ones:

Daemonical Devon

Has anyone heard anything about the Elder
Ones? I found an old book of my grandpa's
that mentioned them alongside normal demons
and stuff. I didn't know what to make of it but
I'd like to learn more. TIA

1989TheNumber:

Maybe its just some older demons? Something
like deava's from Zoroastrianism? They are
much older than Christian/Satanic demons.
More proof that the Abrahamic religions' ideas
of good/evil are bunk. If anything they are pale
imitations of the real deal, and I bet those
came from Persia.

45474Eva:

You are totally ignoring Judaism/Hebrew
mythology, which could be older than that, you
fucktard.

deleted user:

Yeah, I know a little about them. They are the
gods before capital 'G" God was even thought
up by some fucker in a cave. You won't find
out much about them in normal occult texts.
You gotta go to the really esoteric stuff. Think
The Elder Darkness. You know, the book we all
want to read but there's only a few dozen
copies.

There are others too, but that's the one most know. Look, even talking about them is dangerous, I'll say that. Look into the history of Solomon and his signet ring to get an idea of what I'm talking about.

I wouldn't dig too deep into this if I were you. They came from the stars before Earth had even cooled, and they'll wake up when the end comes. Most of the time, you don't have to worry about the Elder Ones themselves, but their kids. Those fuckers are still active and walking around. My money is on most cryptids being them. Shit that live in the forests, in caves. The Loch Ness Monster, Bigfoot, that kind of shit.

Anyway, take the blue pill this time, kid. Don't go down the rabbit hole.

1989TheNumber:

If this shit's such a dark secret, how do you know about it? Sounds like some lizard-people level conspiracy bullshit.

deleted user:

I was in this cult once. I broke away when they wanted me to eat a kid. Made the Son of Sam shit look tame. Like I said, don't look any further. You don't want to end up missing.

There wasn't a lot to work with here, but it seemed to Trey that the deleted user did actually have some idea of what they were talking about. The mention of King Solomon's Signet set off alarm bells in his head, and he wrote that down in his Moleskine for later. That was likely connected to the Fifth Signet. As for the children of the Elder Ones, he was wondering if that was another avenue to go down.

Trey was continuing to type furiously on his keyboard, looking for more records of these "children". The deleted user's post history wasn't available, so he went back to search engines and scrolling through forums and social media groups he was a part of. He barely noticed Sam come in.

"Hey," she said.

"Hey. Becca, go home?" he asked without looking up.

It was almost 1:00. He needed to start getting ready and stop drinking.

"Yeah, she needed more rest. You find anything?"

"I did, actually," he said with a smile. "What if this isn't the work of the Rootmother herself, but one of her kids?"

"Kids?" Sam asked as she sat next to him on the couch.

"Yeah. It's not the most reliable source, but this guy on an occult forum I've used before mentioned knowing about the Elder Gods, and possibly the Fifth Signet. They didn't go into detail, but said that the Elder Ones had offspring that roam around and are more dangerous because we can actually run into them. Ring a bell?"

"The thing that got Granger? You think that's one of Khythk'uhn's kids?"

Trey hadn't seen this monster, but both women got a decent look at it. They said it was tall and lanky and walked on its knuckles like an ape. Becca said it almost looked like a bat if you kept the arms but got rid of the wings. They ran into it in a small clearing, and Granger shot at it. The creature turned on him and tore into the poor bastard before he knew what had happened. Sam and Becca got the fuck out of there before it could do the same to them. He couldn't help but wonder if this was the thing he saw on the road on his drive in.

"We heard the council call Gideon... 'the son'," Trey said carefully. "Maybe he was possessed by one of her children, or was becoming one."

"Or maybe they were wrong, and he was something else entirely," she said, sighing.

"Yeah. It's not much, but it's a start. Still

doesn't explain the dolls, or anything else really, but it does maybe give us a shot."

"How so?" Sam asked.

"We were able to kill the other 'son,'" Trey said. "I bet that means we can kill this one, too."

Trey walked into the Lodge at exactly 1:59. He clocked in before he was officially late and took over for Cindy without many pleasantries. She wasn't very talkative tonight, and that suited him fine. Before coming to work, he had swung through Eaton's and grabbed some sleeping pills. He was hopeful that he could drug himself enough after work to avoid any dreams tonight. There was enough weird shit on his mind—he didn't need to think about his dick getting ripped off again.

Cindy left with a wave, and Trey was alone. The hours ticked by slowly. None of the regulars were showing tonight, which made it even more boring than usual. Trey went into the kitchen and made himself a burger, listening intently for the door. He wasn't sure if he had ever wanted to see a customer this badly before.

Around 7:30, he finally got one. It wasn't a regular, but it wasn't a stranger, either. Herman Stuvland walked in and plopped down at the bar with a huff. The male librarian hadn't come into the Lodge on Trey's shift before. He figured the man for a teetotaler. It seemed that the extra work caused by Becca quitting had won out over any attempts at sobriety, however.

"Outsider," Herman said, "I didn't know you worked here."

Trey doubted that.

"What'll it be, Herman?" Trey asked, all business. He knew that man wasn't going to be a source of information.

"Whiskey," he said. "Straight. Bring the bottle. I've had a day."

"Sure thing," Trey said.

Then a thought formed in his mind. A dangerous one. Trey dropped the bottle on the floor. It shattered with a crash so loud that Jameson came out front to see what had happened.

"Sorry, boss," Trey said sheepishly. "Dropped the whiskey."

"Outta your check," the man mumbled before shuffling back to his office.

Herman looked agitated, but surprisingly held his tongue.

"I'll get a fresh one from the back," Trey said, gingerly stepping over the broken glass and the lake of Tennessee's cheapest.

After passing his mess, he had to stop himself from running into the kitchen. He pulled a fresh bottle out of storage and took the cap off. From inside his pocket, Trey fished out the little box of sleeping pills that he had purchased earlier. Crushing them with the bottom of the bottle, he dumped the powder inside and shook it up.

Returning to the bar, Trey pulled out a glass and filled it nearly double what he normally poured.

"Leaving the bottle for you, sir," he said with a wink. "This'll be on the house if you keep my little mishap to yourself."

Herman nodded and waved Trey away, downing the glass in one gulp like he had been given a large shot glass, and then started pouring himself another. Trey cleaned up his mess and then wiped down the end of the bar, trying not to make it obvious that he was watching Herman.

13

Herman passed out not an hour later, slumping onto the surface of the bar like a man who had just been shot. Trey pretended to shake him just in case Jameson decided to come walking out right then.

"Herman," Trey said, "I think I have to cut you off."

He fished around in the man's pockets until he found his keys: one for his car, one for his house, and one for the library.

"I'm taking your keys," Trey said. "You're in no condition to drive. I'll walk you to your car, and you can sleep it off in the parking lot."

Trey slung one of the man's arms over his shoulder and dragged him outside. By the time he dropped Herman in the back seat of the man's car, Trey was soaked. He wiped the sweat from his forehead and locked the car with a satisfying click. The bastard wouldn't wake up until well after he should be at work the next day. Jameson certainly wasn't going to wake him.

After he got back inside, Trey finished out the remainder of his shift as if everything was normal. A few more people trickled in, but no one commented on the man snoring in the back seat of his car out front. Trey had dumped the rest of the contaminated bottle down the drain so that he didn't drug everyone else who came in that night, which meant they were onto their third bottle of the night. His check was gonna be really short when the inventory came up light.

He closed up the Lodge after Jameson had gone home and climbed into his car, trying to contain his giddiness. Yes, he was supposed to keep a low profile, but how could he miss out on an opportunity like this?

They'll understand, he thought. *Hell, Becca will probably kiss me.*

A few minutes later, he was pulling up in front of the library. No one was out at this time of night, especially not the police, who were now even more short-handed. He tried not to think about Granger getting his guts spilled out by one of the Rootmother's children. It was too fucking horrible to come to terms with. Not because he was particularly fond of Granger, as nice as the guy seemed, but because it was one more stroke of bad luck against his team.

The Backwoods Grindhouse team.

He liked the sound of that. This could be something if he would stop fucking up so badly and earn their trust back. Hopefully, tonight would change that.

The street was dim; the moon was covered in thick clouds, and the streetlights, even on Main, were few and far between. Confident that no one was watching, Trey bounded up the steps and slid the key into the lock. One turn later and he was inside the foyer, surrounded by the paintings of alien landscapes. Illuminated only by his flashlight, he thought they looked even more ominous than before. Were these paintings of wherever Kythkh'uhn came from? And if so, how?

Ignoring his urge to wax philosophical in his mind, Trey pushed on into the library itself. The front desk was vacant, as it should have been. No lights were on anywhere inside the building. That meant McReedy didn't burn the midnight oil at her desk.

Thank Jesus, he thought.

All around him, the bookshelves towered above the shallow sphere of his flashlight like giants. Trey swallowed hard and tried not to look beyond the illuminated floor in front of him when he realized that the shelves were reminding him of the trees in the forest from the night before. The hair on the back of his neck stood on end as he felt like eyes were on him. His pulse quickened, and he started running down the aisles to where the Rare Book Room was.

A few moments later, and he was there.

"Fuck," he whispered. He hadn't thought about the lock on this door.

Trey swallowed hard and tried the key. The door unlocked with a satisfying click. All of the locks in the building had been keyed the same. That in itself was a stroke of luck. Once inside the glass office, Trey shut the door and locked it behind himself.

Ignoring his earlier fear, he flipped the light on in the office so he could see the rows of occult and rare books better. There was the one he had come for: *The Elder Darkness*. The book from the forum post. He slid the leather tome out carefully and laid it on the desk. It was a hefty book, fastened with a metal clasp on the front. Trey twisted a knob, and the clasp came undone. He flipped through the pages and felt his stomach drop.

The book wasn't in English. It looked to be partially in Latin, and possibly something even more archaic. There was no point in taking this back home. He sighed and put the book back on the shelf. Scanning the other spines, he looked for something else that might help.

Trey knew he could only get away with stealing one book tonight. Evelyn was unlikely to suspect a break-in if it was just one missing volume, so he needed to be selective here. *Paganism & Pioneers* called to him again—but he couldn't remember the section about the Green Goddess mentioning any of her offspring. *Revels of the Worm* was there too; it was a title he recognized, but the subject matter he was unsure of. Then he saw a thin volume on the bottom shelf. It was a brown leather spine with faded black letters that read: *Of Daemon's and Their Spawn.* He squatted down and flipped through the book to make sure that it wasn't just a list of Judeo-Christian demons. It didn't take long for him to find the name Khythk'uhn, and he knew that he had found the jackpot.

Moments later and the bookshelf was back in order, the gap hidden by some strategic placement of the neighboring volumes. Then he flipped off the lights and locked the door behind himself. His flashlight clicked back on to illuminate a child staring at him from between two rows of books. A child dressed in pioneer clothing.

Trey nearly pissed himself. Then the child started running toward him. Talking to this kid suddenly seemed like a bad idea, so Trey turned and ran back toward the front of the library. Even though his own footfalls echoed around the giant space, he could hear the pitter-patter of little feet getting closer and closer. Finally, he slammed into the outer door and stumbled down the steps to his car. Only then did he feel safe enough to turn around.

The door slowly swung shut, and there was no sign of anyone chasing him. For the first time that night, he wished that he hadn't used up all of the pills in Herman's bottle.

After throwing Herman's keys on top of the still-sleeping man, Trey returned to Sam's house and shut himself in his room. She was already asleep, so he could avoid the awkward conversation about what a "low-profile" meant until tomorrow. His blood still pumping from the imaginary chase in the library, Trey settled onto his bed and opened the book.

He was thankful that he looked for the name Khythk'uhn specifically, because if he had just given the book a cursory glance, he would have seen mostly familiar demonic names like Alastor, Beelzebub, and Legion. But there were other names inside that seemed more...alien.

Khythk'uhn was one. My'kko'ka, another. They weren't explicitly named as Elder Ones in this book, but the descriptions matched up with what he knew so far about Khythk'uhn.

While the description of the Rootmother and her domains of influence was rather lacking, there was a section on her progeny. His heart leapt. This was what he needed.

Kythk'uhn slumbers beneath the roots of a great forest, yet her kin still slither and creep among the world of men. Not all are known, except to them who have heard the music of the spheres. Herein are those to which I am familiar:

Korshalum- The Widening Maw, Forest-Hunter.

Extorruk- The King of the Stone, Lord of the Ash.

Thy'ar- The Grave Worm, Scion of the End.

Trey rubbed his eyes and read the passage three more times. He wasn't sure that what they were dealing with was one of these three, but he aimed to find out. Korshalum sounded the most promising, as "Forest-Hunter" seemed like it would describe the thing that Becca and Sam had seen. He pulled out a pen and his notebook. He looked at the time, and it was nearly 4.

"God dammit," he said, closing the book.

He needed sleep. By now, the adrenaline had worn off, and Trey felt exhausted. He was out before he even had a chance to put the book away.

14

Becca crawled on top of Trey. He had been lounging in bed, not looking at her, and that just wouldn't do. She pulled the book out of his hand and tossed it to the floor. Her man flushed as she removed his glasses and started kissing her way down his body.

She got to his pants and slowly unzipped them, biting and licking at the skin on his stomach and thighs. Once his pants were on the floor with the book, she grabbed his manhood through his underwear and started to squeeze it with her hand. Becca felt him get hard. She started to touch herself as they both moaned softly. Then she was pulling his boxers off and planning to place him in her mouth.

Slowly, she slid his boxers down. In place of a penis, a large white worm was between Trey's legs. Becca screamed as the end of the maggot opened, dripping a thick mucus on the bed. She looked at Trey's face, and to her horror, it had become the staring face of a doll. Becca scrambled backward off the bed, but the doll reached out and caught her by the hair, pulling her head down toward the worm.

Becca rolled out of bed, hitting her head on her nightstand. The jolt of pain woke her with a start. Her head throbbed, and she was pretty sure that she could feel blood running down her scalp. She didn't need to check her bedsheets to know what those looked like. Instead, she ignored them for now and hopped in the shower.

After she was thoroughly scrubbed clean, she got dressed for work and drank coffee from her leaky mug. It was Tuesday, which was a good thing. Becca didn't want to relive Sunday or Monday, for that matter. The image of Clarence Granger's intestines sloshing onto the ground like someone spilled a bunch of sausage in a butcher shop filled her mind. She dumped the coffee, popped a pill for her headache, and walked out the door.

The ground was tacky outside her house, like she was stepping on soda spilled on the floor of the theater. Unfortunately, or fortunately, she supposed, a thin layer of mist covered everything from her ankles down, so she couldn't see what the stickiness was from. After her dream last night, she decided that was for the best.

Her car started on the third try, and she was off, driving out of Fallen Lilly Trailer park and heading for Bridgette's Boutique. She didn't mind this job, but it was a far cry from working at the library. While Becca enjoyed making recommendations to library patrons and even shelving books, she couldn't stand the "oohing" and "ahhing" that came with clothing retail. Becca didn't like pretending that every piece of clothing looked good on every customer. In fact, as she knew most of these people her entire life, she felt like they had earned a bit of honesty from her.

Bridgette felt differently. Becca had found herself in trouble more than once for telling someone that the outfit they were trying on wasn't flattering. While her friends had appreciated it, her boss hadn't.

"If I hear you do that again, Rebecca," the woman had said, "I'll be forced to let you go."

This was one of the few places she felt safe working at, so Becca pulled up her big girl pants and became a liar. Now everything fit just right, nothing made someone look fat, and no, these clothes weren't going on sale next month. What did people expect from the only clothing store in town? Did anyone really want to risk driving to Portland or Hood River and decide halfway through trying on skirts that their wrists needed to be opened up?

She stepped inside the quaint little store and went to work, straightening clothing on hangers and making sure the mannequins looked as natural as possible. Bridgette could be heard humming from the back of the store. Even if she was a saleswoman first and a person second, at least she was more bubbly than Evelyn had ever been.

Becca realized that she hadn't so much as seen her old boss up close since the night she had almost been sacrificed. She wasn't sure what she would do if she did. Yes, she had known the woman was a nasty old bitch, but taking a girl she had known forever and strapping her naked to a rock? Get real. But that's exactly what she had done.

Maybe I should listen to Trey more and take the fight to them, she thought.

She really wouldn't mind shooting Evelyn McReedy or Eaton Marsh in the face. Pain welled up in her palms, and Becca realized that she had been clenching her fists so hard she was nearly bleeding. She took a deep breath to steady herself.

"Everything all right, miss?" a man asked.

Becca jumped.

"Shit!" she exclaimed.

Then she turned, blushing, to see the man named Malcolm standing in front of her. She had been so lost in thought that she hadn't heard the bell on the door. Thankfully, Bridgette was still in the back of the store and hadn't heard her curse in front of a customer.

"I'm so sorry," she said. "You just startled me...Mr. Bryant."

"Malcolm, please," he said with a nod. "I only like to flick your boyfriend shit. You're fine."

"He's not..." she trailed off.

"Ah, coulda fooled me. I figured you two were fucking."

Becca blushed again as Malcolm laughed.

"Okay, maybe I like to flick everyone shit. Now, I'm here for some clothes."

"Of course, duh," Becca said with a forced laugh. "Let me walk you over to the men's section. Do you know what you wanted to look at in particular?"

"Actually, I wanted to go to women's, please."

Becca paused, then put on her best retail smile.

"Of course! Daughter? Wife? Girlfriend?"

"Does it matter?" Malcolm asked, his smile fading.

"N-no, I just wanted to make sure we went to the right section."

"Grown women, please. Nothing fancy, just a couple of shirts and a few pairs of jeans."

Becca led the man over to the women's section, where he quickly flipped through T-shirts and jeans. He didn't pay any attention to the styles, instead checking sizes before setting them back down. Finally, he had a few of both, and Becca was checking him out at the register.

As Becca handed him his receipt, Malcolm said, "Tell your boyfriend to be careful. With two cops missing now, he's not as safe as he thinks he is."

"How do you know about—" she began, but Malcolm quietly shushed her.

"Don't go looking for trouble, and it won't go looking for you. Isn't that the saying? Well, it might be true for white folks, but it was never true for us. And here, it isn't true for anyone. But him poking around is only gonna make things worse. Believe me, you three will want to ride out the storm that's coming, not jump out in front of it."

Then he walked out of the Boutique without another word.

"Who was that, dear?" Bridgette asked, finally coming to the front.

"A friend...I think," Becca said.

"Fantastic!" Bridgette said. "I'm going to go back to unpacking. Let me know if either mayoral candidates come in. With the election just a few days away, I expect them both to come and buy some new clothes for their speeches."

Becca nodded and watched as Malcolm crossed the street and disappeared from view.

When she got home that evening, Sam and Trey were waiting for her. Confused, she waved for them to follow her into her trailer. It was a mess again, as she hadn't been expecting company, but they had grown used to that by now. As they all sat down, Trey's eyes drifted to the bedroom and the bloody sheets on the bed. He didn't say anything about it, but his eyes were sad.

"Don't you have to work tonight?" Becca asked.

"I did, but I called in this time," he said.

"So..." Becca trailed off, tapping her fingers on the table.

"I—" Trey began.

"This motherfucker," Sam cut him off, "drugged your old coworker Herman and broke into the library last night. *Without permission.*"

Trey flinched at her tone. It was clear that he had already gotten an ass chewing before this.

Becca rubbed her temples as she reconsidered why she was developing feelings for this stupid man.

"Well, I guess you picked the right time to do it," she quipped. "There aren't many cops left to come after you."

"All right, now tell her what you found," Sam prompted, her voice much calmer.

"First, I want to apologize," Trey said. "I saw an opportunity, and it's not like I could loop you two in on it at that moment."

"Save it," Becca said. "Get to the reason it was worth it, please."

Trey pulled out a small brown book from his bag. Becca didn't immediately recognize it, but from the looks of it, she expected that it came from the Rare Book Room. The title was *Of Daemon's and Their Spawn*.

"This book talks about what I suspect are a few of the Elder Ones. But more importantly, it catalogs some of their progeny...their kids. Khthk'uhn specifically has three listed. Thy'ar, Extorruk, and Korshalum. This is important because the book claims that while the Rootmother is stuck sleeping beneath the earth, her children are still roaming the surface. And I think you two ran into one of them two nights ago.

"Korshalum is known as the Widening Maw and the Forest-Hunter. It is described as a pale beast in the shape of a 'long man' that hunts for flesh in the forests near its mother. I don't know exactly what it means by 'long' in this context, but I'm betting it means tall and long of limb. Like the thing that killed Granger."

Becca shivered and nodded.

"What else does it say?" she asked.

"Well, not a lot more. Each entry is kinda weak, to be honest. This author, a 16th-century monk named Johannes Schröder, was compiling information from a variety of fractured sources. Hell, I don't even know how he had any information about a monster on a continent that he might not have even been aware of."

"Okay," Sam said. "So this gives us an idea of what is doing this, but we still don't have a how or a why. It didn't mention dolls, nor did it say how to kill this thing. So we're barely better off than we were yesterday."

"Worse, actually," Becca said.

"How so?" Sam asked.

"Our friend Malcolm came to the store today," Becca replied. "He bought some women's clothes, for whom I don't know; he was kinda cagey about it. But he did say that we need to keep our heads down because things are about to get worse. And he also knew Granger was 'missing'. I don't know how the fuck he would know that, the rumor mill hasn't even made it to Bridgette yet."

"Fuck," Trey said, staring at the table. "I knew he had something to do with this. But what? I don't think he's Fifth Signet."

"Me either," Becca said. "I think he's on our side, but I can't figure him out."

"One problem at a time," Sam said. "Right now, I'm not as worried about this guy's cryptic messages. I am worried about this sasquatch-motherfucker in the woods killing kids and leaving fucking dolls around."

"Oh shit," Trey said.

"What?" both women asked in tandem.

"There wasn't a doll left of Granger," he said. "I mean, not that we've heard of. Like you said, Becca, most people don't even know he's missing yet, outside of the other deputies. Both Ron and Mary's dolls were left out where they were found almost immediately."

"What are you saying?" Becca asked. She tapped the table nervously.

"I don't think Korshalum is the doll-killer."

Sam slammed her head on the table and sighed.

"But I do think it's one of the other two," Trey said.

"And why is that?" Sam asked without lifting her head.

"Because that little kid was in the library with me. That means we're getting close."

Becca got up and brought each of them a beer. She looked at Trey expectantly.

"Well, spit it out, detective," she said. "Which one is it then? I imagine you read about them both."

"Neither of them is connected to dolls, at least not as of this writing, which makes sense as china dolls like these weren't around back then." Sam winked at Becca, and both women tried to stifle a laugh. Trey and his tangents. "But Thy'ar is also called 'the Grave Worm'. There isn't much in terms of description here, but...that night when we were chasing the kid, I woke up with maggots in my hair. Another name for maggots is—"

"Grave worms," Sam finished for him.

Becca felt sick.

"My dream last night," she whispered. "You... uh...had a maggot for a dick."

"Ah," was all Trey said.

15

Willard had been sitting at the table, staring at the doll of Ezekiel for most of the day. His eyes were vacant, and he ignored all attempts by Henrietta to coax him back to the present. When Joshua finally awoke in the afternoon, Willard seemed to return to the be with the living, until the boy shared that he had no memory of what had happened to his brother, and then he was back to his previous, glassy-eyed expression.

The search party had broken off only an hour or so after Joshua and the doll had been found. The hope had been that the recovered boy would be able to point them in the correct direction, but Henrietta had known from the moment she laid eyes on the doll that her other son was dead. Throughout the day, there were periodic well-wishers who stopped by; she sent each of them away in turn with a humble thanks, hoping that none had looked inside her home hard enough to see Willard. Though she didn't expect anything different, she was saddened by Eliza's absence—though Henrietta wasn't certain that she would have been able to control herself if any of the Winslow clan showed up on her doorstep today.

As the woman of the house, and with one child still living, she knew that she would need to put on a brave face today for the sake of her family. Ignoring her catatonic husband, Henrietta busied herself around the house, making sure that Joshua was well-fed and spent time practicing his letters with his Bible. She kept the fire stoked all day, filling the small cottage with the comforting smell of smoke. The window shutters she kept closed, however, forcing them to rely on the fire and candlelight to see. Something inside forced her to keep Jackson Point shut out as much as she could.

Dinner came and went with little fanfare. Joshua and Henrietta ate stew at the table while Willard quietly turned the doll in his hands and seemed not to realize that they even existed. When that sorry affair was over, she ushered her son back into the room where he and his brother slept. She tried not to look at the other bed in the flickering light as she pulled back the blankets for Joshua.

"Mother," the boy whispered as he was being tucked in, trying not to draw the attention of his father. "Why isn't daddy looking for Ezekiel?"

Henrietta chewed her lip. Even though she had yet to share what she knew to be true with Willard, his instincts had very likely led him to the same conclusion.

"He is just tired, that's all," she whispered. "You boys gave us quite a scare, you did. We will find your brother, and everything will go back to normal."

"Promise?"

Henrietta pretended that she didn't hear him. She kissed his forehead and blew out the candle near his bed, leaving enough shadow that she could pretend both of her boys were safe in their beds that night. As she walked past the table, Willard's hand suddenly shot out and grabbed her arm. Henrietta saw the cords of her husband's neck tighten, and his eyes focused on her as if it was their first time seeing.

"You know what *this* is, don't you?" he hissed, tilting his head at the doll.

"I—" she began.

"Sit DOWN!" Willard shouted, slamming a palm on the table.

The woman started to shake when he finally

released her arm, and she lowered herself to the table. She had never seen him like this before. Willard had never been a harsh man, not to her or the boys. But now…his face was twisted and alien, like it was simply a mask of the man she had once loved.

"What is this?" Willard asked.

"H-Hyrum Winslow makes these dolls," she stammered. "He's a dollmaker."

"And why is there a doll that looks exactly like our son?"

"Because Hyrum killed him."

Willard clenched the doll in his fist so hard that it broke. Shards of the porcelain must have cut into him, as blood now seeped between his fingers onto the table. The thirsty wood sucked up her husband's blood like a leech, leaving a crimson stain on its surface. Willard's eye never left Henrietta's, however, and the mask that made up his face was cracked with a predatory grin.

"How?" he whispered.

"Things that Eliza said to me," she answered. "I told you he wasn't a good man, that I thought he harmed Eliza and the boys? Well, I also think he killed their first daughter, Winifred. He made a doll of the dead girl that the family keeps…a doll just like this one. They won't talk about it, but I just know something happened…" Her voice trailed off. Then she was wracked with great sobs, the entire day's worth of emotions rushing out all at once. "I think he killed Ezekiel because I interfered with his family. Willard, *please*! Forgive me!"

His fist opened, and the broken doll fell to the table in a white and scarlet heap. He reached out and touched her cheek with his bloodied hand, and for a brief moment, the mask was gone and the real Willard had returned.

"I won't believe it," he said softly. "Our boy is still out there, and I aim to bring him home. This isn't your fault, Etty. I should've dealt with Winslow the day I told him off."

He pushed out his chair and grabbed his rifle from above the mantle. Henrietta watched the door close behind him in silence. It wasn't until she felt Joshua crawl into her lap that she forced herself to stop crying.

The next morning, Henrietta opened the door to their house and found a bundle of cloth on the doorstep. She lifted it up and unwrapped the small object within. The doll of Willard hit the ground and shattered as her shriek shattered the morning stillness.

16

"What about our kids?" someone from the crowd shouted.

"This has to stop!" yelled another.

"Don't look for trouble, and she'll leave you be," a man beside the trio whispered. "Just a'watch where ya dig…"

Trey, Sam, and Becca were standing together in a small crowd watching what constituted the single debate between the mayoral candidates. A small stage had been erected in the Ansel Public Green behind the library. The election itself would take place inside the community center, but that was still a day away. An eternity in Jackson Point.

Brent Doherty waved his hands in a placating gesture to quiet the crowd. He was dressed not unlike the last time Trey had seen him, though his suit today was a more subdued grey than the pinstripe blue of before.

"I hear you," Brent said, drawing out the words as if they each held multiple syllables. "It has been a hard year for this town, for all of us. Normally, we keep to ourselves. We look out for one another, give the forest the respect it deserves, and that's that. Some days, *she* takes her price, but mostly we are left alone. This year has been different."

"Why?" The crowd shouted. "What have we done? What will you do to stop it?"

Brent scanned the crowd, and Trey felt the man pause as he passed over the *Backwoods Grindhouse* crew. A thin smile formed on the man's lips before he spoke again.

"I think what has happened is a natural consequence of allowing outsiders to pollute our town. We are a close-knit people, but in the last few years we've strayed from our values and welcomed newcomers who would destroy what we have built."

Becca squeezed Trey's hand. He tried not to look around for fear of seeing the hungry eyes of a lynch mob staring back at them. Beside him, Trey felt Sam shift as she reached into her coat, no doubt gripping her pistol for reassurance.

"Brent, I think that's enough fear-mongering,"

Melanie Thatcher said, stepping forward to the center of the stage. Brent, to his credit, gave a curt nod to his opponent and stepped back to let the woman speak. "We cannot place the blame on any one person. That is not who we are. I look out into this crowd, and yes, I see new faces. Faces of folks not born here. And that isn't something to fear. We know she brings people to us—for what purpose we aren't always sure—but I pray to the Good Lord that we won't think ourselves so high and mighty as to assume that purpose."

A murmur of agreement and a smattering of applause rumbled through the crowd. Melanie smoothed out the pleats in her skirt as she waited for what they all knew was coming.

"And what of the old ways?" an old man asked. "We used to deal with crime one way—right there on those same boards you are standing on. We had our justice in this town. In my day, no child-killer would be allowed to—"

"Mr. Miller," Melanie said firmly. "We don't know what happened to Mary Simmons, and as for all those taken from us last year...the forest provided its own justice."

"Did it?" Miller asked. "We've had no sign o' the sheriff—or her lackey now—in months. The way I see it, Nancy Tench was the one to do it, blaming it on the Rootmother herself to shake our faith! And now she's gone and taken Mary Simmons to do lord-knows-what!"

Trey bristled at the accusations, but Becca kept him in check. They needed to keep a low profile still. This was enemy territory, through and through. That wasn't going to change any time soon.

Up on the stage, Melanie looked dumbstruck. What could she say that wouldn't piss off one side of the town or the other? Brent took the opening and returned to the fore, his face a mask of seriousness that seemed that it would befit a eulogy more than a mayoral debate.

"I agree with Mr. Miller," he said. "There are more skeletons in the Tench's closet than any of us would care to admit. Indeed, that's why I am planning on instructing the next sheriff to begin a complete investigation into Nancy Tench and her whereabouts, as well as bringing the mill under the control of the city."

There was an uproar in the crowd now. Trey was momentarily thankful that the talk had moved on from demonizing outsiders like himself, even if it meant dragging the Tench family through the mud. Their hands hadn't truly been clean, either, he supposed.

"You can't do that without council approval!" Melanie exclaimed, standing nose to nose with Brent. "Your family has always wanted the mill.

The estate is being processed, as we all know, and the ownership will be passed on to—"

BANG!

Trey jumped at the sound of the gunshot. He looked around in a panic, but the crowd was gone. No longer was the podcaster standing outside on Ansel Green, but instead, he was in the mayor's office holding the proverbial smoking gun. Arthur Tench was sitting at his desk, a red flower blooming on his shirt. His eyes were glassy, but they gazed right at Trey.

"You could have stopped this," the dead man rasped. "You had the chance to end this. All you did was delay the Rootmother's return. You should have killed them all. Instead, you only killed me."

"N-no," Trey stammered. "I killed Abner. I got one of them."

"Did you?" Tench asked.

"I killed him!"

"Jesus Christ," Sam hissed. "This is not the fucking time, Treyton."

Both Sam and Becca grabbed Trey and dragged him out of the crowd, many of whom watched them go with baleful eyes. Trey's legs felt like jelly. Dumbly, he let the women lead him away from the green for at least a block before they finally came to a stop.

"What the fuck was that?" Becca asked. The venom in her tone stung.

"I-I don't know," Trey replied. "I was thinking about Tench, and then I was back in his office, right after I shot him..."

"Well, now half the town heard you say that you killed someone," Sam sighed. "Not like you haven't been advertising that on the podcast, I suppose."

Trey felt like he was going to be sick. The PTSD was bad enough, and now it seemed like his night terrors were blending together with his waking moments. Had he really been having some kind of trauma-induced flashback, or had he actually been transported back to the moment he had killed a man?

"You don't think Abner could be alive, do you?" he asked.

Neither woman answered him. They were too busy watching a small boy staring at them from between two houses. The boy was the same one who had attacked Trey in the library, and here he was watching them in broad daylight.

"Who are you?!" Becca shouted. "What do you want from us?"

"You mustn't go into the basement," the boy replied. "Father hates that the most. Mary, she went into the basement."

Sam lunged at the child, but the boy ducked

into the yard behind the house before she could reach him. The trio spread out to look around the block for him, but the kid had vanished without a trace.

"We let this settle for a day or two, and then we go back to looking at houses," Sam said when they finally gave up. "Now we know we need a house with a basement. It's time to get you each your own gun. I have an idea about that."

Night rolled around without any further sightings of the kid. Trey had just finished his shift and was sitting alone in his car, eating a cold Happy Burger. The girls would be waiting for him to pick them up soon so that they could enact Sam's plan. But first, Trey wanted to take another look at something that had been bothering him since that morning.

He drove up the overgrown road that ended at the gates to the Ansel Mansion. His headlights cast shadows from the wrought-iron gates over the front of the great house like prison bars. Nothing seemed any more amiss than usual, but Trey knew in his gut that this centered on the Mansion. It had to. Maybe there was a basement here?

No way in hell Ron would've taken an order to

come to this place, though, Trey thought. Still, this Oregon Trail/Children of the Corn reject kid had to have come from somewhere, and Trey knew from experience that the Ansel home wasn't completely tethered to the present. Feeling a momentary swelling of courage, Trey honked his horn three times to see if anything popped out to greet him. Thankfully, nothing did.

Trey flipped around and headed back toward Sam's place. He would have to convince them to come back during the day and do another search again this week. They wouldn't like it, but that had helped them last time—surely it would again.

❀

It was nearly four o'clock when Trey killed the engine in front of the Simmons' house. Sam had known Michael to be quite the sportsman and gun aficionado, and none of the trio had seen anything resembling gun cases in their car the day they left town. In the rush to escape Jackson Point, Samantha hoped that Michael Simmons had left a least a few firearms behind.

After a few long minutes sitting in the dark, they crept from the car around to the back of the house. The yard here wasn't fenced, though it was mostly secluded from prying eyes by a few large sycamore trees. When they reached the back door, Trey was prepared to pry it open with the crowbar they had brought. That proved unnecessary, however, as the door hung ever-so-slightly ajar already. The wood around the dead-bolt had been broken, like someone had kicked it in.

Trey and Becca each raised a flashlight while Sam lifted her gun. She cursed under her breath but pushed her way inside all the same. Inside, the house was in complete disarray. It looked as if everything left by the Simmons family had been thrown about the house in a frenzy. Shattered plates, broken picture frames, and articles of clothing covered the floor in the living room and kitchen. Trey felt his chest tighten. Did someone know they would come looking for guns?

The trio swept each room in turn, checking to make sure that the previous intruder wasn't still waiting for them. When they were sure that the house was empty, they relaxed a bit and started their search. Sam went to check the primary bedroom, hoping that Michael kept at least some of his guns in a safe in the closet—what they would do if he had left the safe locked, Trey wasn't sure. Becca was looking in the laundry room, and Trey was left picking through the least likely places: the bathroom and Mary's room.

The bathroom looked less rifled through than the kitchen and family room had been, but the medicine cabinet still swung ajar. The room smelled of stale bleach, but seemed relatively clean. The linen closet held nothing besides a few towels and neatly folded sheets. Trey swallowed hard and tried to tamp down the emotions that he was afraid would swell up when he went into Mary's room. He almost didn't want to check, but they could leave no stone unturned.

He pushed the door open and peered inside. Everything was pastel pink and unicorn-themed, from the curtains to the bedspread. The bed looked as if it had been searched by the intruder as well, for what Trey could only guess.

On the wall were pictures colored with crayons and finger paints. Trey half expected to find an image of a worm, a pioneer boy hidden between the unicorns and cats. He nearly laughed at the idea that this would work out like some low-budget horror film. He walked around the bed, planning to check underneath it after he looked in the dresser. Trey didn't even make it past the foot of the bed before his light fell on a cluster of rocks on the floor. They were arranged in a near-circle, with a pair of dolls sitting in the middle of them. His pulse quickened.

Even if he hadn't studied the pictures he had taken, the pattern of those stones had already been seared in his mind last year: The Elder One's Crown.

Trey knelt down near the rocks and looked to see what Mary Simmons had been trying to tell him. One of the dolls was naked and tied with a string, while the other stood over her with a pair of plastic scissors in her hand.

"Trey?"

"Fuck!" Trey shouted, jumping to his feet and spinning his light on Becca. "You scared the be-jesus out of me."

Becca smiled slyly at him.

"Sorry, you just looked so serious," Becca said. "What were you looking at, any—what the hell is that?"

She peered over his shoulder at the crude display. Trey had a moment of discomfort and tried to shield the dolls with his body.

"Is-is that supposed to be me?" she whispered.

"It's just a coincidence, Becca," he said, grabbing her hand. "There is no way this little girl knew about what happened to you."

"Yeah," Becca said. "Let's get out of here. Sam found some stuff under the bed in the other bedroom."

Back in the kitchen, Sam had a few handguns

and a shotgun laid out on the table, along with several boxes of ammo.

"This is everything he left that has shells or brass here. I suppose we can get the few other things and try and get some ammo from Jackson's, but I don't think the attention is worth it. Everybody grab something and let's get the hell out of here."

"Agreed," Becca said.

Moments later, they were carrying everything out to the car. Trey tried to push Mary's room from his mind. The rot in this town ran deeper than he had even imagined.

17

School and most of the businesses around town were closed the next day in honor of the election. Sam stood in line with dozens of others to drop a makeshift ballot in the box at the far end of the community center. She had marked the box for Melanie Thatcher, not that she expected the vote to mean anything. The city council was in charge of counting the ballots, of course, so the word "impartial" was nowhere to be found. On principle, however, Sam would still vote for Melanie over Brent. Hell, she would have voted for Trey over Brent, and Trey seemed to be getting dumber by the day.

Truth be told, Brent or Melanie being mayor would make little difference to the actual goings on in Jackson Point. The council, and therefore the Fifth Signet, controlled everything. Tench only had the means to push back against them because of who his family was— only the mill and the sheriff's department helped too. Now with him dead and Nancy missing, there was no way anybody could stand against the council. This was a figurehead job. Brent getting elected would stroke his ego, but little else would change. Melanie would probably follow Tench to the grave by the end of the year if she actually tried to enact radical policies.

Like everything else in this town, it was a facade. And like every other time, Samantha found herself playing along with the charade, because that was the safest option.

Back at her place, Trey and Becca were still sleeping in from the late-night adventure. Sam was too restless to stay in bed. Even though it had been her idea, crawling through the house that had, until recently, been home to a vibrant little girl who was now likely dead, hadn't done much for her nerves. She hoped that after Kevin and...Gideon, things would have calmed down in this hellhole. At least enough for her to start looking for signs of her grandfather again, but nothing settled with Trey around.

And that pissed her off.

That's it, she thought. *When this is over, I'm kicking his ass out. He can keep doing his dumb show, and he and Becca can ruin their own sheets without actually fucking, but—*

"Excuse me? Ms. Moore? Sam?" a familiar voice asked from behind her.

Sam turned and saw Cynthia Anderhoff behind her. Kevin's mother hadn't wanted much to do with Sam after Kevin's funeral, not once her *association* with Trey had become widely known. Being friends with the only town real estate agent would be helpful for that particular problem, right about now. Too bad the woman blamed Trey for the death of her son.

"Cynthia, hi," Sam said, forcing a smile.

"Who'd you vote for?" Cynthia asked, forcing an awkward laugh. "I'm kidding. I'm sure you're a Brent fan."

Why in god's name is she doing this? Sam thought.

"I...uh..."

"It's okay, I'm voting for Melanie too," Cynthia whispered. "Don't tell my mother that, though. Mrs. Best is happy that another old family can fill the Tench void. It's all about consistency for people her age."

"That's what I hear."

"Look, I know we haven't spoken since...in a while, but I wanted to let you know that I don't hold it against you."

Sam instinctively took a step backward. She'd

heard this white-woman approach before, and it stank just as much as it did even in the normal world.

"What do you mean?" she asked.

Cynthia's eyes went from bright to flint in a flash.

"Keeping that *outsider* in your home. You were always such a good person, always looking after the outcasts. That's why Kevin liked you so much. It makes sense that you'd bring his killer into your home when the whole town turned their back on him, too."

"Trey is many things, but he didn't kill—" Sam began, trying to keep her voice level.

"He might as well have! He started this whole mess!" Cynthia hissed. "And I heard what he shouted at the debate yesterday. He said he killed *him*. Who else would that be? Arthur Tench?"

Samantha gripped her ballot until it was wadded up like a used tissue. She tried to keep a smile on her face, but could only manage a pained grimace.

"I don't know what you're hoping to accomplish, *Cindy*, but I don't like the insinuation that I would ever take in someone who did that to Kevin. In fact," Sam began as she leaned in close and whispered as quietly as she was able. "We took care of the people actually responsible. *I* killed the man who did that to Kevin, and I'm willing to do so again to protect the people I love."

Cynthia looked conflicted for only a moment, then she was all smiles again.

"Don't be a stranger, now," she said with a perfunctory wave.

Moments after being left alone, Sam found herself in front of the ballot box. The crumpled ballot wouldn't fit through the slot, so she awkwardly smoothed it out like a shitty dollar at a vending machine and fed it in with a mumbled apology.

Outside the community center, she wrapped herself tightly in her coat and started back for home. Standing not far from the stage where the debate had happened the day before, Brent Doherty stood chatting loudly with a crowd of voters. Melanie was nowhere to be seen.

The walk home was quiet, and Sam was actually grateful that she had foregone her car this morning. She doubted that she could drive with the waves of anxiety that were assailing her. Was it the venom from Cynthia that rattled her, or the fact that she had used the word love to describe her relationship with Trey and Becca?

Sam clenched her fist around her revolver for comfort. She no longer left home without it, and now she wasn't sure that she would ever be able to again.

The afternoon rolled around before Becca and Trey got out of bed. Thankfully, they weren't covered in blood when they shambled out to the kitchen for coffee and toast. Sam offered to drive them down to the election, and they both sleepily agreed that would be for the best. Once the voting was done, they could begin their search for the house where Ron's fateful pizza delivery happened.

In the car ride to the community center, Sam considered telling the pair about her run-in with Cynthia, but decided that Trey didn't need the extra baggage right now. Sparing him discomfort at her own expense pissed her off more. By the time they parked, she could have shot him in the face for breathing wrong.

It's not me, she thought. *It's the town. It makes us this way.*

After a few deep breaths, she followed them back into the community center—if for no other reason than to keep them out of trouble. The line was practically non-existent now. The polls would likely be closed in the next half hour. Sam expected that Brent would be announced as the mayor before dinner. After dropping their ballots, the pair returned to her, still rubbing the sleep from their eyes. Trying to tamp down her annoyance, Sam led them back outside and right into the path of Brent Doherty.

"Why, Ms. Moore, a pleasure seeing you here today," he boomed in an all too jovial voice. "I hope you voted with your conscience today."

"I sure did," Sam muttered.

Brent's eyes fell on Trey, and he smiled in a predatory way.

"My, my, the fabled Treyton Savage of *Backwoods Grindhouse*," Doherty said. "I'd wish you the same, but I doubt you have a conscience."

Sam instinctively reached into her coat for the reassuring feel of the pistol grip. It seemed like every conversation in this town was laced with menace ever since Ron died.

Maybe that asshole pizza guy was keeping the whole thing together, she thought.

She would have laughed at her own joke if Trey hadn't opened his dumb mouth.

"So, you're a fan of my show?"

"I wouldn't say that," Brent replied, examining his fingernails. "But I do keep tabs on everything that goes on in this town...and I must say, your fanciful tales about last year—about the city council and *Khythk'uhn* are very troubling."

Each member of the trio was taken aback by his brazen use of the Rootmother's actual name. There didn't seem to be a soul in town who didn't hide behind euphemisms when talking about the Elder One.

"What are you getting at?" Becca asked.

"I'm just letting Mr. Savage know that when I'm mayor, I won't be as lenient towards his meddling as my predecessor."

Then Doherty nodded and walked on, whistling as if he didn't have a care in the world.

"He knows he's gonna win," Trey muttered. "The bastard knows he's gonna win."

"You just figured that out?" Sam asked. "Come on, let's get going before it gets too late. If we leave now, we can be back in time for the 'results' to be announced."

Still realizing that she hadn't seen Melanie that day, a pit started to form in Sam's stomach. She had a sinking feeling that the truce with the Fifth Signet was about to be ignored.

18

Trey once again sat in the backseat for this batch of exploration. He cradled a shotgun on his lap while flipping through notes in his Moleskine and consulting *Of Daemons and Their Spawn,* which he had brought with them. There wasn't much to glean from that book that he hadn't already discovered, but he was loath to give up scouring it for something else. It was all they had, really.

"Maybe we should break back into the library," he thought aloud.

"What did you say?" Becca sounded incredulous. Sam simply tapped her fingers on the steering wheel.

"Together, I mean," Trey said, closing his notes. "Look, I'm hitting a wall here with the one book I did take. Maybe the three of us together could look through the restricted books until we find something else. I'm not saying we steal any-thing—especially not if fuck face becomes mayor. Just a quick…and thorough peek."

Neither woman responded for what seemed like an eternity. Then Sam finally said, "Let's table that for now—but I'm not saying no. We're running out of time here, between the election, the Anderhoffs, the dolls…"

"Whoa, whoa, whoa," Trey said, leaning for-ward. "What about the Anderhoffs?"

Sam turned the car down Wacum Road, pointedly not making eye contact with either Trey or Becca. She cleared her throat a few times before reaching into her coat, where Trey knew she had her gun. It was a troubling nervous tic that she had developed recently, and it made him uncomfortable.

"While I was in line to drop off my ballot this morning, Kevin's mom confronted me about giving you a place to stay. The guy who killed her son."

"Fuck," Trey whispered. "Sam, I'm sorry."

"Yeah, it sucked, but I threatened her, and that's that, at least for now."

"You threatened her?" Becca asked. "Like, you told a grieving mother you'd blow her brains out, or what?"

"You make me sound like a royal bitch when you put it like that," Sam laughed.

Trey couldn't join in. The knife twisted in his gut as he thought about Kevin hanging from that tree, half eaten by his gym teacher. His mother had every right to hate Trey for that, especially after he beat the shit out of Kevin right before he died.

"Is she still just holding me responsible, or does she think I actually ripped out his guts and chewed off his feet?" Trey asked.

Outside the car, the trees hemmed the road, brown and green fingers trying to close around them. Trey snapped his gaze away from the outside and looked back at his shaking hands while he was waiting for Sam to answer. His fingers traced the trigger on the gun and thought about how easy it would be to put the barrel in his mouth...

"The latter, unfortunately. Your outburst at the debate didn't help. Shouting 'I killed him' when people are talking about missing kids isn't a good look, outsider or no. Look, I only mention it because Jackson Point was basically content with overlooking us these past few months, and I think that time has passed. This Malcolm guy, Cynthia, Brent...it's too many people sniffing around us at the same time for comfort.

I think we're in danger again. I don't think your stalemate with the council is gonna last."

Trey grunted in agreement and went back to looking out the window at the houses that they drove past. So far, none look abandoned, but Becca had mentioned that this road went back farther than some of the others. After Wacum, they would have to do Davis, which Becca would likely sit out for obvious reasons. As far as Trey knew, she hadn't gone back down that road since her family had died.

"What about this one?" Sam asked as she pulled into an overgrown driveway.

Two rusted-out cars sat in the yard, and the front door swung ajar on the wind. At first glance, it didn't look much different from the last house they checked—when they had that run-in with Malcolm—but what made this one promising were the small windows at ground level, denoting some kind of basement.

"Okay, so if we see this pioneer kid, do we shoot him?" Becca asked.

Trey tried to glare at her, but failed spectacularly. Becca laughed with a snort, which made Sam laugh too. Trey lightened up a little then, but his finger kept twitching toward the trigger on the shotgun. He couldn't honestly say that he wouldn't shoot the kid the next time he saw the creepy little bastard.

They climbed the porch and stopped just short of the door. Sam had shown each of them how their guns worked before they left, but she made each of them do a final check to ensure they were loaded and the safeties were off.

"We don't split this time," she said. "Too dangerous with all three of us armed. One squeaky board and I'll become the victim of a hate crime."

Trey chuckled until he saw that Sam wasn't smiling. He really wasn't used to being the butt of jokes about racism.

With that, Sam kicked the door open and shone her flashlight inside. After making sure that the front room was clear, she stepped inside, gun raised. Even though things had been tense with Sam lately, he couldn't help but be incredibly attracted to her at this moment. And, no matter how much he liked Becca, he hadn't ever had a dream about Sam biting his dick off.

Inside, the house was even more musty than the last one, with piles of leaves and other debris in each corner. The shafts of sunlight illuminated a thick cloud of dust kicked up by their passing. Trey fought back sneezes and wished that they had brought masks. The walls were smudged with a dark substance that could have been mud or blood, and the entire house had an earthy smell.

The group traipsed through the foyer and

down the hall into the kitchen. The buzzing of flies greeted them just as it had in the last house. Though there were no signs of spoiled food this time, maggots frothed at the base of the walls like a sea of surging rice. Becca covered her mouth as she started to retch beside Trey.

"I think we're in the right place," he whispered. "Grave worms."

"What do you think we do if we run into this bigass worm?" Sam asked as she tried the door that seemingly led to the basement.

"Well, fire worked last time," Becca said. "Maybe we can just shoot the bastard. It's just a worm, right?"

Trey nodded, but his mind was racing. He didn't have a plan, like last time. They didn't have clues from an old journal telling them the monster's weakness. They just had guns and the hope that they could blast their way out of a problem. Seeing as that had worked so well for him in the past, Trey wasn't thrilled about their chances.

The door creaked open, revealing a concrete stairwell that went down into the basement. Trey shuddered a moment before taking the lead. Sam tried to protest, but he silenced her with a look. This was his mess, and he wasn't going to endanger them more than he already had.

After rounding the corner halfway down, the steps turned to old, sagging wood, and the walls were just as likely to be brick as dirt, it seemed. All the while, the scent of rot and soil assaulted them. Trey knew that they were in the right place. The question now was just what they would find at the bottom of these steps?

When he reached the bottom, the basement opened up before him more like a massive cavern than the bottom floor of a house. Other than the few windows that they had seen from the outside, there was no source of light, and no visible wall except the one the windows were set in. In between the final creaking sounds of Sam and Becca's descent, Trey could hear a faint wet sound like something was writhing in the muck.

He pressed ahead, casting his light left and right in slow motion. No matter which direction he pointed, the light was swallowed up by the distant blackness. This basement, it seemed, was never-ending. Trey felt his feet slipping on something wet, even as the writhing sound grew louder. Still, he refused to look down at the ground.

"Sweet Jesus," Sam said from behind him. Clearly, her self-control had not been so strong.

"Maggots?" Trey asked.

"Maggots," Sam confirmed.

Then Trey's light caught the glimmer of

something white ahead toward the ground. He was forced to lower the beam of his flashlight, revealing the undulating floor of grave worms that he suspected was below them. Fighting back the urge to scream, he pressed on to the white object ahead.

The object turned out to be *many* objects. Several hundred porcelain dolls lay scattered in a circle, free from the writhing maggots. Trey could tell without close examination that each doll was unique, a marker of someone who had been killed in Jackson Point in the service to Thy'ar and Khythk'uhn.

"How is this possible?" Becca whispered. "That many people haven't gone missing lately. This would be like half the town!"

"Just like what we faced last year, this has happened before," Trey replied. "This may have been happening for hundreds of years, and no one knew..."

A streak of morbid curiosity overtook him, causing Trey to smash one of the closest dolls with his foot. Sure enough, fresh blood dripped from the shards of porcelain even though the doll looked to be decades old. No sooner did his foot return to the patch of maggoty ground outside of the doll graveyard than Trey heard a much louder noise than the writhing beneath them. A loud slithering sound echoed from further into the darkness. As the sound grew louder, the entire cavernous basement began to shake.

"Run!" Trey shouted. "This was a fucking stupid idea! Run!"

They all spun, slipping on the slick floor of white threads beneath them. Trey shook a handful of the maggots from his arm after catching himself, and then sprinted back toward the steps. Sam and Becca reached them first, bounding up the stairs two at a time. A loud crack followed by a scream signaled that Becca had broken through a rotten board. Trey lifted her from behind and pushed her up in front of him. All the while, the slithering sound was getting louder, and the smell of something rotten grew stronger.

"What the fuck?!" Sam shouted from above. "The door's locked!"

"You should have listened," a child's voice echoed from above. "I warned you to stay out of the basement!"

"Who are you?" Sam asked. "Open the door!"

"It's too late now. And you didn't even find the right house."

Sam was throwing her weight into the door, but to no avail. Dust and dirt rained on them from above, as the shaking became more intense.

"Move!" Trey commanded, raising the shotgun.

Sam slipped down the steps beside him as he squeezed the trigger, blowing the door apart around the handle. Ears ringing, they forced their way upstairs and ran from the house. There was no sign of the kid, but even up here the ground continued to shake.

"Don't stop!" Sam shouted as she sprinted toward the car.

The tires were spinning out, and the car was racing down the road before they even had time to finish closing their doors. Behind them, the old house collapsed inward as if a giant sinkhole had opened under it. It wasn't until the trees parted to reveal Jackson Point that anyone broke the tense silence in the car.

"Yeah, you can shoot the kid," Sam said.

19

A much larger crowd than had been there all day was gathered outside the community center by the time they parked the car. It had been decided that Becca would be the best option for finding out the election results without drawing too much negative attention. Even with her connection to Trey, Becca was still well-liked in Jackson Point, or at least pitied enough to treat her halfway decently.

First, she composed herself in the mirror while Trey and Sam sat silently, each no doubt grappling with the horrors from the preceding minutes. Becca had suggested that they leave the election for another day, but for some reason, her friends liked getting bad news, it seemed. When she was done, Becca slid out of the car and gently pressed the door shut, as if closing it too loudly would bring the crowd's attention onto her. Based on how intently they were gathered around the door, she supposed that wasn't likely to have happened.

When she made it to the back of the human wall, a few dainty apologies allowed her to slip between folks until she was closer to the front than the back. The doors of the community center were open, but a stern-faced man she recognized as William Horvitz stood like a sentry while members of the voting committee—Evelyn McReedy and a few other council members—finished the tally. After a few minutes of trying to ignore the smell of body odor just as much as the nausea that was a result of the adrenalin wearing off, McReedy herself walked out and patted William on the shoulder.

"It was a close election!" she shouted. Becca felt that the woman's voice sounded frailer than usual. "Even so, Brent Doherty has won the election! The council will certify the results and swear him in this evening!"

I don't know why I had to stand here for that, she thought.

Becca tried to push her way out of the crowd, but suddenly felt the crush of people tighten against her. Her pulse spiked as she thought back to last autumn, when she was nearly sacrificed by the very elders of this town. How many others could be in on it this time?

"Excuse me," she squeaked.

The closest people to her seemed not to have heard. She had to be imagining this. There was no way that this many people could turn on her so quickly.

"Anyone know where Brent is?" someone asked.

"I'm surprised a man like him wouldn't be here with a speech in hand!" someone answered.

Becca pressed again, and this time was able to break through. On the far side of the crowd, she doubled over, losing control of her breathing. She had never felt so claustrophobic in a crowd before. It was almost like she was trapped in that basement again, with that *thing*, slithering up behind her. Just as she was preparing to make her way back to the car, someone from inside the crowd pulled on the back of her shirt. Becca turned to see the boy who had locked them in the basement standing sandwiched between the legs of two adults who didn't seem to even notice that he was there.

The boy put a finger to his lips as if to shush her, before shoving a small object wrapped in burlap into her hands. Reflexively, Becca stumbled backward from the boy, who had already vanished into the crowd. She didn't need to unwrap it to know what it was. A scream started to form in the back of her throat. She was trapped out here with Sam and Trey back in the car. Trapped in broad daylight.

"What have you got there?" a voice asked.

Becca was too afraid to turn and look at the speaker. It was as if the boy had paralyzed her with his touch.

"Rebecca? Becca White?" the woman asked. "Are you alright?"

"Y-yes," Becca lied. "I...I don't know what this is. Some boy handed it to me, just now."

Melanie Thatcher stepped into view and gently took the burlap from Becca's shaking hands. She unwrapped the thing and gave out a cry that would have put Becca's to shame. The crowd wheeled to see what the commotion was. Moments later, men and women both were ex-claiming in confusion and horror.

"What do you know about this?" Melanie de-manded of Becca once she had regained her composure.

Becca felt herself shaking her head furiously, but her body seemed miles away, tied to the rock in the Elder One's Crown. Melanie stuck the doll with the likeness of Mayor-Elect Brent Doherty in her face, her fingers clutching the porcelain so hard it threatened to shatter.

"I'll ask again," Melanie demanded. "What did you do to Brent Doherty?!"

Becca's savior didn't turn out to be either Trey or Samantha, but rather the last person in the entire town that she would have expected: Evelyn McReedy.

"That's quite enough, Ms. Thatcher," McReedy said. "I doubt poor Ms. White had anything to do with this peculiar...development." Her eyes slid over Becca like they belonged to a lecherous old man. "Everyone! It is at the behest of the council that you return home for the evening while we try and locate Mr. Doherty. In the event that he cannot be found, the office of the mayor will pass to Ms. Thatcher. Come, Melanie, we have much to discuss."

The crowd parted for the women, who walked back into the community center while William closed and locked the doors behind them. Becca stood still as a statue while everyone walked past her. It didn't matter if they ignored her or gave her a slim smile; she felt naked in front of them, all the same.

Becca knew she wouldn't be able to sleep by herself that night, so she opted to come home with Sam and Trey again. She was sitting on the couch, crying into Trey's shoulder. She had never felt weak like this before, but today had shaken her. Sam paced in front of them, loosely holding a beer bottle by the neck between her fingers. Becca hoped it wouldn't fall. She wasn't sure that her nerves would be able to take it.

"What the actual fuck is going on?" Sam asked no one in particular. "There's no way that slimy bastard wasn't Fifth Signet. So why did they take out one of their own?"

"Maybe they didn't," Trey mused.

This even got Becca's attention. She lifted her head to look at him with an expression that she hoped was more charitable than it felt.

"Elaborate," Sam said.

"We don't know that this killer, this kid, whatever he is, is Fifth Signet," he began. "Yeah, we assumed that because it seems like more sacrificial killings to the Rootmother, but what if it's not? What if this kid, or whoever is behind this, is just feeding people to Thy'ar for shits and giggles? The dolls, the victim pattern, everything about this feels much more chaotic than last year. I don't think the cult nor the council is behind this."

Sam plopped down in her usual chair and put her head in her hands. If she was feeling anything like Becca was, it was somewhere between confusion and hopelessness.

"Okay," Becca said, wiping her nose. "Let's pull on this thread for a moment. Do you really think the council would just 'sit one out' while one of *her* children is running amok?"

"They controlled Gideon," Trey said, "but that doesn't mean they actually have any power over the real Elder Spawn. They don't control the Rootmother, so why would they control her actual offspring? Hell, that's probably why they called Gideon 'the son' in the first place, to make themselves seem higher up in the food chain than they actually—"

"Please," Sam interjected, "stop using his name. Jesus Christ, Trey, you aren't the only one of us to suffer through some fucked up shit this year!"

"I didn't say—" he began.

"Actually, you did!" Sam shouted, standing. "You are clearly suffering from PTSD from dying and killing folks. We all know that. But when have you checked on us, huh? When have you asked me how blowing my boyfriend's brains out felt? Or how it felt to let a man put his mouth on me who had just eaten a fucking child?"

Trey was pulling away from Becca and sinking into the couch.

"And what about her?" Sam continued. "Becca was strapped naked to a fucking rock, and they did lord knows what to her before we got there. You think you can white knight this shit, and we'll just be fine? You think you're the only one who gets to shoulder the trauma? Goddammit, we all know about a fourth-dimensional goddess that will one day annihilate the planet, and you're the only one in pain?! I need a walk."

Sam grabbed her coat and was out the door before Trey or Becca could manage to come up with any response. Trey turned and looked at Becca. His eyes were red, but he was doing his best to hold the tears back.

"She's just upset," Becca whispered. "Today was...rough."

Trey shook his head.

"No, she's right. I haven't been a good enough...friend, to either of you. I'm sorry. Do... do you want to talk about what you're going through right now?"

"Maybe tomorrow. Tonight, we need to figure out our next move. I'll go get her before she wanders off and becomes worm food."

Becca pushed herself up and rushed out the door without a coat or shoes. She didn't need to give Trey time to try and stop her. Harsh as she was, Sam was right, and sometimes Trey just needed to shut the fuck up.

It didn't take long to catch Sam, nor did it take long for Becca to regret the lack of shoes and a coat.

It's February in the Gorge, she thought. *What am I doing?*

"Sam!" she called.

Her friend jumped, her hand already in her coat, clutching the pistol underneath. Another thing Becca should have thought to grab. Ahead, there was a bench sitting under one of the few streetlights here. Sam motioned to it, and they both sat down. Sam quickly gave her coat to Becca, ignoring the other woman's protests.

"You need it more than me," she said. "I have shoes at least, and I'm not dressed like a bimbo right now."

Becca gave her a playful shove and pulled the coat on, lifting her knees to her chest and zipping it around them. She knew that she looked ridiculous, but at least she wouldn't freeze to death. They sat in silence for a few minutes, slowly moving closer to each other as the cold air set in.

"You didn't remember shoes or a coat, so I imagine you didn't bring a flask either?" Sam asked with a wry smile.

"Nope. I was just trying to get out of there before Trey chased after you. I knew if that happened, either he'd end up dead, or you'd never come back."

Sam lay her head on Becca's shoulder. Her cheeks began to glisten from the tears that crystallized on them.

"This is all too much," she said at last. "I know he means well, but he's had his head so far up his own ass since he got here, and if he doesn't figure it out, it's gonna get you and me killed. Even if that doesn't happen, we'll come out the other end of this—if there is another end—hating each other...and I don't want that, Becca..."

"I don't either. I'll talk to him—"

"Fuck him," Sam sighed. "I don't want to lose either of you, but fuck him right now. We agreed that we were gonna run this case—Jesus Christ, don't say it—and it's time we run it."

Becca squeezed in tighter. Something about having Sam this close kept most of the cold away.

"He might be right, though," Becca said. "About the council not being behind this. I don't know why they would take out one of their own like that...and give me the evidence right there in front of everyone..."

"In front of Melanie," Sam mused. "Maybe we're looking at this the wrong way. Melanie was nowhere to be found when any of us voted, but she suddenly shows up right after the kid? What if they were both Fifth Signet? We know the entire election was a farce anyhow. Maybe Brent wasn't as tractable as Melanie. Maybe there was some kind of internal power struggle, and she won?"

Becca chewed on this for a few minutes, trying not to think about how inviting Sam seemed at this moment. She had read about trauma-bonding before, and she didn't want to do something to jeopardize their friendship—or whatever *it* was she had with Trey.

"I'm following you. Whatever is going on, they know more than we do, whether they're directly involved or not. I hate to be the one to suggest something rash, especially after today, but I think we need to take a page out of our boy-toy's book and break back into the library. Not a peek like he suggested. No—we take it all. We burn what we can't use."

Sam sat up and looked at Becca with a sly smile. The light of the street lamp cast a silver sheen on her dark skin. Becca realized that she couldn't smell Sam anymore, and it made her ache.

"Becca White, I can't believe you," Sam laughed. "We still need to figure out how this creepy little kid fits into this."

"I know just the genius to put on that problem."

20

Church was the last comfort that Henrietta allowed herself, yet this Sunday was the first that she considered skipping since Willard's death. The following Wednesday would be the 4th of July, a day that she normally would have marked by baking an apple pie for the boys, preparing a picnic, and seeing if Willard could procure some fireworks. This year, she expected to sit with Joshua alone in their house, alternating between crying and praying.

After a sleepless night of indecision, Henrietta realized two things: first, she wasn't going to get through this without the Lord, so she needed to go to church, and second, that she finally had the courage to confront the Winslow family.

As loath as she was to leave Joshua alone, even to use the privy, Henrietta decided that she didn't want him to see her enraged in the house of God. Instead, she made him porridge and extra honeyed biscuits to keep him occupied, and promised him more sweets just so long as he stayed in the house. Given everything he had been through these last few months, the boy was happy to oblige. On her way out, she locked the door behind herself and tucked the key into her hair under her bonnet. There was no reason to take any chances.

Lord, forgive me, she thought.

The crowd that filtered into Forest's Hope this morning was larger than it used to be. A few more children had gone missing since Ezekiel, causing the people of Jackson Point to lean on their faith to survive. People went missing here all of the time, they said, but maybe if they just prayed to God or the Rootmother more, the forest would stop taking the children. Henrietta knew better. It wasn't some heathen monster that had taken her son and husband from her—it was an incredibly wicked man.

She shuffled into the back, trying not to be noticed. The other sawyers' families had rallied around what little was left of the Frock family, helping with food and covering the payments to the Tench family so that she didn't lose the house. Their good Christian charity had been a balm in the beginning, but lately had become a millstone around Henrietta's neck. They couldn't support her and Joshua forever, so she would need to find a suitable income or remarry—neither of which she wanted to do. All she wanted was to stay by her surviving son and see Hyrum hanged.

Shepherd Cabot droned on about forgiveness and faith in hard times. Henrietta hardly noticed. Instead, her eyes bored a hole into the back of Hyrum Winslow's skull. The murderer was sitting in his usual place toward the front of the church. He was there with Alastor and Malthus and...Eliza was nowhere to be seen.

While the two had not spoken since that day, the Winslow woman had told Henrietta to stay away from her family; she had never missed a day of church, no matter how sick she had seemed. Something must have been wrong, either with her or their baby. For a moment, Henrietta was no longer a grieving mother and widow, but a friend struggling with the fear that something evil had befallen Eliza. Then she hardened her heart when she thought of the porcelain doll of her son.

When it was time for communion, Henrietta went and knelt before the altar and took the Lord's sacrament as she always did. It was when she was walking back to her pew, however, that she noticed Malthus was holding a doll that looked just like his mother.

"No," she whispered. Then she was shouting, "Murderer! Murderer! Hyrum Winslow killed my son and husband! He has taken your children! He has killed his own wife!"

The church erupted into pandemonium then, with dozens standing and shouting, while some of her husband's friends gripped her by the shoulders and tried to keep her from attacking the Winslow Patriarch. Shepherd Cabot tried to bring calm to the situation, but it was too late. Several crying women threw their hymnals at the Winslow family, and a large man knocked Hyrum to the ground. Then others rose up, shouting in the family's defense, pressing the others back.

"She's hysterical!" one cried. "There is no evidence!"

"The woman is mad!" shouted another.

"Kill that bastard who took my Charlie!"

"Not in the house of God!"

"Rootmother, take him! She won't mind the blood in 'ere!"

It quickly became a brawl that wouldn't have been out of place in a Boston tavern. Candles were knocked over, causing flames to lick hungrily up the walls. Women and children ran out screaming as smoke and shouts filled the air in equal measure. In the midst of the chaos, Henrietta stood her ground, staring directly into the eyes of the devil that took her family from her. She hardly noticed when she was carried to the fresh air beyond.

Hyrum Winslow and his children had escaped the madness somehow and proceeded to lock themselves into their home. None had come in or out in the following two days. One man who had approached the front door had even been shot at. As for Henrietta, she had also been confined to her home, though not of her own accord. While Forest's Hope had been saved, she was still being charged with inciting a riot and was told to expect "the forest's justice" very soon.

Those two days had been some of the longest of her life. She spent the time cleaning every inch of her home more than once. When her knees ached and her fingers bled, she decided that it was time for Joshua to hear the Bible read aloud from cover to cover.

They were about halfway through Deuteronomy when there came the first knock at the door since her imprisonment. It was Wednesday now, the 4th, and she expected the town to be engaged in revelry, not thinking about the crazed widow and her son. She stood from the table and smoothed out her dress before approaching the door.

"Keep reading," she said gently to her son.

When she opened the door, she was not greeted by the local deputy who had been set to guard her house, but rather a group of men from the mill, all of whom had murder in their eyes. She recognized most of them: Miles Perkins, Theodore Gaunt, Tracey McMillan. All men who had worked with her husband. It was after briefly looking them over that she saw the deputy restrained behind the men.

"My boy went missin' last night," Miles said. "They found a doll bearing his likeness this morning. We aim to put a stop to this, here an' now. Tell us, Etty, is it really Hyrum Winslow doing this?"

At first, she thought she would cry hearing that another child had met the same fate as her son and all the others, but instead, she let out a cackle that would have once left her feeling ashamed. Even with half the town after him, even after killing his own wife, the devil couldn't be satisfied. The men didn't say anything to stop her fit of laughter, but she could tell that they were none too pleased with her flippancy.

"Yes, I'm sure," she said, finally. "He is a doll-maker. Those hellish things he leaves behind are of his craft. Before my boy, he had killed his own daughter, and Willard…" she paused as her laughter turned into sobs. "Willard went to confront Hyrum the night he was taken. I told the deputies, but they didn't listen."

"We will get you justice, Henrietta," Tracey said.

"You heard her!" shouted Miles. "Grab guns, axes, whatever you've got that'll get us into that monster's house! Tonight, he hangs!"

Then the mob was gone, leaving no sign of its passing except a bound and gagged deputy. Henrietta closed the door on the man and returned to the table.

"Was all that true, Momma?" Joshua asked.

"Back to your reading, son," she whispered, wiping the tears away. "Turn to chapter 32, verse 35, and you read it to me."

The boy obliged, flipping a few pages ahead in Deuteronomy.

"To me belongeth vengeance and recompence; their foot shall slide in due time: for the day of their calamity is at hand, and the things that shall come upon them make haste," he read aloud.

Henrietta smiled and embraced him. Tonight, she would finally be able to sleep.

21

You didn't even find the right house.

The words that the pioneer kid—they really needed a better name for him—taunted them with from behind the locked door nagged at Trey all night. He had slept alone this time, dreamless, thankfully, but he felt that there was a growing wedge between him and his two partners. Sam and Becca had shared a room, which Trey told himself was for Sam's sake.

They were out for coffee this morning, leaving him at the computer to do some research. It was Friday already, the week had decided to jump ahead suddenly, so Trey had a longer shift coming up. School and the Boutique were still closed, however, as the mayor situation had the town on edge again. He sighed and rubbed his temples. For some god-awful reason, he had decided to abstain from day drinking after what happened last night, and he was already regretting it.

You didn't even find the right house.

Even though he was sitting at his computer again, his mind kept wandering back to their multiple run-ins with the boy. Maybe Trey's gut was right, and they should have been checking the Ansel Mansion. Ron probably did die in the house they investigated yesterday, but that didn't mean that was the monster's lair.

Do giant worms even have lairs? He thought.

Trey grabbed his backpack and pulled out his Moleskine, Ansels' Journal, and *Of Daemons and Their Spawn.* He was nearly starting his own library of occult tomes. Once, that thought would have excited him. Now, he felt those books were a tremendous weight. He flipped through Ansel's Journal for any mentions of Thy'ar, or graveworms, and came up short. If this had happened before, like Trey suspected that it had, it must have been after Ansel's death.

Likewise, his searches for Thy'ar online proved fruitless. He wasn't sure why he would have expected anything more than that, but Sam and Becca put him on this, and he didn't want to let them down.

"Who the hell are you?" he asked aloud.

Taking another approach, Trey pulled up the archives of The Oregonian, which had articles stored all the way back to 1850. While in the past he would have preferred to do this in the library, that was no longer a safe option, so he had to hope that the digital records were complete. Even with this handicap, the podcaster was finally back in his element. He typed "Jackson Point" into the search bar and went to work reading every single article on record, from the death of Frederick Ansel forward.

Soon, he found something of note from 1906 which gave him pause:

Friday, July 6th, 1906

White Man Lynched in Logging Town

Two days ago, while the rest of the nation celebrated the 130th anniversary of our nation's founding, the sleepy logging community of Jackson Point was the site of a vicious case of mob justice.

While details are scarce, as the people of Jackson Point are known to keep to themselves, reports state that a prominent member of town, a man named Hyrum Winslow, was killed after several children were reported missing. Winslow, a renowned doll-maker, was set upon by a savage group of loggers and sawyers who blamed the man for killing the children over a period of several weeks.

Local law enforcement denied comments on the particulars of this lurid case, but it is unlikely that any charges will be brought forth, lest the whole town be put on trial.

Trey whistled and kept going. Nothing else mentioning dolls came up in his search of local papers, so he decided to follow up on Hyrum Winslow instead. Thirty minutes later, and he was looking at an obituary from 1894 for one Winnifred Winslow, daughter of Hyrum and Eliza. Winnifred had been missing for months and was finally declared dead at the behest of her father. Not only was a picture of the poor, raven-haired girl included, but also the picture of a porcelain doll that Hyrum had made in her likeness.

While it took considerably longer, Trey eventually discovered one final mention of the Winslow family, including the names of their two sons: Alastor and Malthus.

"Jesus Christ," Trey whispered. "I think I've found you. *Backwoods Grindhouse* isn't done yet."

Scooping everything back into his bag, Trey raced out the door. This couldn't wait. He would have to catch the girls before they came home and fill them in. Now they had something. If they could look through town records and find out which house was the Winslows', Trey knew that they had a shot at ending this. Once they figured out how to deal with a giant worm-deity, that is.

22

Trey didn't make it more than two steps out of his car when he was shoved from behind into the alley at Fernando's. He instantly regretted leaving the pistol inside his backpack instead of figuring out a way to keep it in his coat. Pain blossomed from his forehead as he was slammed into the wall of the café. Trey tried to turn and fight back, but instead found his arm twisted so hard that he thought it would break.

It's not so easy if they aren't a high schooler, he thought darkly.

"Stop fighting me, white boy," a familiar voice said.

"Malcolm?" Trey asked.

"Well, it certainly isn't Brent Doherty."

His grip relaxed, allowing Trey to turn around—and to be able to rub his surely bruised forehead. Malcolm looked worse for wear, like he hadn't changed in several days and had been roughing it in the wilderness. Likewise, his usual sardonic smile was replaced with a grimace.

"What the hell was that?" Trey asked.

"I needed to move fast, and I can't be seen," he said. "Sam's house is being watched, as is Becca's, so I couldn't show up there. Once I saw you pull up, I knew I had to move fast. If you were smart, you'd be armed, which is why I was a little rough with ya. I didn't want you to get spooked and—"

"Commit a hate crime," Trey finished dryly. Malcolm didn't laugh.

"I see that stress hasn't improved your humor, or your ability to navigate race relations," the other man said.

If his head hadn't already hurt so much, Trey figured that he would have felt embarrassment. Instead, he was just annoyed.

"Actually, that was Sam's joke. I just—"

"Stole it."

"Yeah."

Malcolm shifted uncomfortably on his feet, looking over his shoulder in both directions before saying anything. A car drove by, causing the man to press up against Trey for a moment until it was out of sight. When he stepped back, he looked genuinely embarrassed for a fleeting moment. Then the moment was gone, and he was back to business.

"I told you to be careful, didn't I?" he asked.

Trey nodded. "And I have been."

"Not from where I'm standing. Look, kid, I'm gonna level with you for once. No jokes, just man to man. This town has always been a powder keg, and now someone has gone and lit the match. With the Mayor-Elect dead and his replacement getting sworn in right after accusing Becca White of murder, things are about to go off. I'd say as soon as tonight. If this was a normal place, I'd say get the hell out of town. But since that's not an option, I recommend you do what I'm doing and find somewhere to hide out where no one will look for ya."

"What's going on? Why do you know so much?"

"It's not my place to say. That's not me being cryptic, hell, that's not even me not trusting you. That's me not breaking a trust, got it?"

Trey didn't, but he nodded anyway.

"There, I've delivered my warning. Now you can do fuckall and ignore me, as I'm sure you will. If that's the case, that house I caught you snooping around in has something you might need."

Malcolm pulled up his hood and started briskly walking away.

"I thought this wasn't one of those stories where the native guy looks out for the white guy!" Trey called after him.

"I'm not the one looking out for you!" Malcolm shot back.

Trey stayed in the alley for a few moments, trying to make sense of what was going on with that guy. Finally, he gave up and rounded the corner into the café. Sam and Becca were sitting at a booth in the back, talking and laughing like everything was normal in their lives. Trey almost hated to break it up.

Almost.

* * *

"So, does he just get off on only telling us half the story, or what?" Becca asked.

"I think he was sincere when he said he couldn't break a trust," Trey replied. "I didn't get it at first, but I don't think he's working alone. In fact, I think he might know where Sheriff Tench is."

Sam took a long sip of coffee. It seemed like she was struggling to look at Trey. He hoped he was imagining it. He liked them both too much to lose either one of them.

"That would explain why he came in and bought women's clothes," Becca said. "She was probably the one hiding out in the house next to his, too. But why wouldn't he say that?"

"So it didn't end up on the internet," Trey answered.

Sam looked so shocked, Trey was sure she was going to drop her coffee. She looked around the room once and then stared really hard at Trey, somewhere around the bruise on his forehead.

"How hard did he hit you?" she asked. "Did you just admit, all on your own, that you have been a little too open on the podcast, thereby putting all of us in danger?"

"To be fair, we did tell him that days ago," Becca giggled.

Trey put his hands up, more to shush the laughter than anything.

"Yeah, yeah," he said. "Right or wrong, I imagine that's the reason. It's hardly a secret if you start blabbing to everyone."

Sam went back to sipping her coffee with a grunt of agreement. Trey picked up his own cup and tried to enjoy the aromatics as much as possible. The smell would have to be enough—he had decided that his head hurt too much to put anything into his body at the moment. When he was done, he set the still-full cup back down and pulled out his notebook.

"Now, back to business," he said.

It only took him a few minutes to bring them up to speed on what he had found. They both agreed that the pioneer kid was likely one of the Winslow boys, though how that was possible none of them could say. Trey told them that he had originally thought it had been the Ansel Mansion that they needed to return to, but he was glad to have been proven wrong.

"So," he said, finally. "What do we do to get records like that? I take it my library plan is still off limits."

"Actually, no," Sam said. "The committee decided to go ahead with that idea."

"Ah," Trey said, smiling. "After my run-in with Malcolm, I think tonight would not be the best time for that."

Then there was a commotion toward the front of the café. A woman Trey didn't recognize ran inside and started shouting at the barista. There were only two other groups inside, but all of them stopped talking to listen to what the woman was saying.

"They found another doll!" she exclaimed. "Justin Waters this time! My cousin, Cassandra! My cousin! What the hell is happening! Is this what she wants? Like last year? Is it?"

The barista, evidently named Cassandra, came around the counter to hold her sobbing friend. Everyone else went back to their coffees and private discussions like nothing had happened. It was Jackson Point, after all.

"It has to be tonight," Sam said. "We can't let this go on a moment longer."

Trey decided his earlier idea had been a bad one, and he quickly started downing his coffee. It wasn't a beer, but it would do in a pinch.

"I need to swing by the Lodge and beg for my job," he said, "because I'm gonna have to take a few mental health days."

23

Herman fell backward as the door busted his nose with a wet crunch. His pitiful whimpering sounded exactly as Becca had hoped it would. He had always been a cruel, nasty little man, and she had wanted to hit him for a long time. She was the first one through the door, her gun leveled at the bloody mess that was his face. He continued to writhe there on his puke-green shag carpet, seemingly not yet recognizing his assailant.

"Keys, Herman!" she shouted. "Now!"

"Mmecca?" he gurgled through his hands.

"Keys, asshole!" Trey commanded.

Sam shut the door to Herman's house behind them with a deliberate thump. She pulled out her revolver and slid the hammer back slowly, right where Herman could see it. He started to cry. Becca almost felt sorry for him—almost.

"You know," Sam said, squatting down and placing the barrel of her gun in Herman's groin. "We'd be better off killing you. Can't risk you telling McReedy about us taking your keys."

Herman was shaking as he lowered his hands from his broken nose. A bloodied finger pointed at the key ring on the wall. Trey unhooked the library key and slid it into his pocket. Then he dropped the fallen man's key ring onto the floor. With a twist of his neck, he motioned Becca over to him. She leaned in so he could whisper directly into her ear.

"I think this is working," Trey said. "He probably thinks we're gonna shoot him as soon as I'm done talking to you." Becca nodded solemnly, making sure that Herman caught her eye. Sam dug the gun into him to return his attention to her. "Are you sure he isn't Fifth Signet? We might be better off..."

"I'm not sure, but even if he is, he's too much of a coward to say anything."

"Fair enough."

They all knew that they would be the first, and likely only, suspects for the break-in, but they didn't need Herman sounding the alarm too early. That meant scaring him into thinking they would actually do more than rough him up. No matter what she thought of him, Herman was still innocent until proven otherwise.

Becca stepped back around Herman before placing her foot right on his chest. Sam stood back up and followed Trey out to the car. "Don't take too long," she said.

"P-please, Becca," Herman pleaded. "You don't have to do this."

She pointed the gun at his head and placed her finger on the trigger. Herman cringed and turned away, as if he could melt into the floor; he was crying again, big wet sobs that caused blood bubbles to come out of his nose. After getting her fill of his misery, she put the gun away and stepped off of him.

"Remember this," she said. "You lost your keys. Dropped them outside the library—whatever bullshit you want to spin. But you have no idea who took them. If you rat me out, I'll make sure you're nourishing the roots long before they find me."

Then she was out the door and jumping into the car with a wicked smile on her face. This was turning out to be more fun than she expected.

This time, they parked around the corner from the library. At Becca's suggestion, they were taking the employee-only back door that rarely saw use. They would be much less likely to be seen this way—not that they expected anyone else to be out at this hour. The air was thick with freezing fog, which caused the sidewalks to be slick. They each had to balance and slowly waddle toward the back door as if they were trying to cross an ice rink. Thankfully, the distance wasn't very far, and they got there without any major falls.

I'll be happy when spring comes, she thought. *Assuming we're alive then.*

When they made it to the top of the stairs, Becca stopped short. A brick was wedged in the doorway, keeping it slightly ajar. All three of them pulled their guns out of their coats.

"Looks like we won't be alone," she whispered.

"Do we call it off?" Trey asked.

"No," Sam said firmly. "Not after fucking up Herman. We need to act, now."

Becca nodded, and for the second time that night, she was the first through the door. Inside was one of the dimly lit back rooms that was used for storage. The room was bathed in a faint orange glow from the incandescent bulb that flickered overhead. She sighed as she realized how far behind Herman must have fallen on the maintenance duties.

"I'd have replaced this," she muttered.

"What?" Trey asked, stepping closer to her.

Sam shushed them and pointed ahead. Unlike the room they were in, the hallway beyond, which connected to several more storage rooms before opening to the back of the library, was dark. They had no way of knowing if the library's other after-hours visitor was lying in wait for them, and they couldn't risk alerting them with flashlights.

Becca tried to fight off the shaking of her hands as she stepped into the dark. She could see a dim white halo at the end of the hallway, which told her that at least some lights were on. That halo became her lifeline as she crept ahead, one foot in front of the other. The smell of paper and dirty carpets wrapped around her. It was nostalgic, in its own way. Though she hated Evelyn McReedy and Herman Stuvland, she missed her job—she missed books. In a perfect world, she could run this place by herself.

Maybe not by myself, she thought.

Though she couldn't see them, knowing that Trey and Sam were behind her filled her with enough courage to make it down the rest of the hall. The walls fell away to be replaced with row after row of books. They were toward the back of the library, by both the stairwells to the upper level, as well as the periodical section. Overhead, the wooden signs that denoted the sections swung on their chains in an imaginary breeze.

Then she saw the source of the light. McReedy's Office, otherwise known as the Rare Book Room, was for some reason lit. Unfortunately, that was one of their two destinations. The other was the town records, which would be far to their left, in the back corner. The books seemed to be more pressing, and they needed to see who was already there, so she led the group in that direction.

Becca had gotten used to sneaking through the library in circuitous paths between the shelves to avoid the watchful gaze of her old boss from the glass box from which she viewed her fiefdom. She relied on that skill now to avoid being seen by whoever had snuck in before them. Each row served as a barrier, which was a blessing and a curse now that she thought about it. Her ears strained to hear the pitfalls of a child chasing after them like Trey had experienced during his last nocturnal visit. Fortunately, there was no sound beyond her own ragged breathing.

Finally, she brought them right to the rear of the glass room, separated from it by only one row of books. Oddly, a few scattered volumes lay on the floor as if they had been pushed from the other side. Becca tried to ignore her librarian's urge to fix them. They crouched and nodded at one another as she signaled how close they were to their destination. They would creep around the corner and try to see who was in there before storming the door.

What if it's Evelyn? She wondered.

They had assumed the library would be empty, as it should have been. If they ran into a member of the council now, it would mean that they would no longer be safe. It would mean that they would have to actually use these guns. As tough as it made her feel to hold, Becca hadn't even fired one before. Last fall, Trey had killed two people, though one technically came back, and Sam another. Becca hadn't been forced into that situation yet, nor did she want to be.

She tried to think of all the kids who had gone missing, replaced with little porcelain dolls. She thought of those murdered last year, eaten by the Gideon-thing. She thought of Jenni. Suddenly, murder didn't seem so hard.

After one final deep breath, Becca rounded the corner. She had to bite the back of her hand to stop herself from screaming. The back glass of the Rare Book Room was splattered in varying shades of crimson and scarlet, all surrounding a sizable hole that cracked the glass. It was clear that someone's brain had painted the rare books, but whose?

Becca was so stunned that she didn't realize

Trey and Sam quickly rushed past her, keeping low to avoid standing level with the windows that wrapped the office. She gathered herself as best she could and followed them around to the door.

Inside the room, Evelyn McReedy sat at her desk with her head slumped backward over her chair. Her glasses hung around her neck from their turquoise chain. A faint, wet dripping noise could be heard coming from inside the room.

"Jesus Christ," Trey whispered. "What the hell?"

"We have been two steps behind someone this whole time," Sam said.

"Nance?" Trey asked.

Sam shrugged.

Becca pushed past them and collapsed into the seat that she normally would have sat in while getting an ass chewing from the very woman who was now a corpse. Though this very woman had tried to sacrifice her last year, seeing her like this was overwhelming. It was one thing to make Herman feel her anger after years of his disgusting behavior toward her, and quite another to literally see through a hole in Evelyn's skull. To add to her dismay, many of the books were covered in gore. Some she would have loved to take.

"We need to go," Sam said.

"What about the books?" Becca whispered.

"And the records?" Trey added.

"We need to go, now!" Sam urged. "It looks like we did this. Herman will think we did this. We have to get out of here."

Trey pulled Becca from the chair and dragged her out of the room behind him. She looked back at the woman who had put her through hell in more ways than one and felt nothing.

24

Trey drove them back to Sam's house in silence. When he asked to have the keys, she surprisingly didn't argue. Everything seemed to be slipping away from them now. There was no way they could get out of this. Even if the Fifth Signet didn't come after them, the sheriff's department surely would. Even scared for his life, Herman was unlikely to keep quiet after finding out that his boss had been murdered on the same night that he was beaten up for his keys.

When he pulled back up to the house, he put Sam's car in park, but didn't turn off the ignition. Both women looked at him quizzically.

"We're fucked," he said. "No two ways about it. We. Are. Fucked. Not only will we get blamed for killing McReedy, but we didn't find the

Winslow house—or a way to stop Thy'ar. That means this continues. People keep dying, and hell, maybe his mom wakes up, and the world ends.

"The way I see it, that leaves us with only a few options. None of them good. I've had the feeling that the Ansel Mansion ties into this, somehow. It seems to be the focal point of so much crazy shit, I don't know. But there *is* something there, and I intend to find it tonight... alone."

"No!" Becca shouted.

"Absolutely not," Sam said. "Are you fucking crazy?"

Trey shook his head.

"You can't talk me out of it, and you can't come with me. You two need to stay here. Pack some shit up and get ready to go on a moment's notice. If I find a way to stop this, great, but we'll still need to hide out somewhere once they find McReedy's body. If I don't come back...well..."

The car was silent for a few long minutes.

"You don't have to do this," Sam said. "I know I've come down hard on you these last few weeks, but that's because I've been scared. Not just of getting hurt, but of losing either of you."

"Love you too, Sam," Trey said.

"Fuck off."

"What about me?" Becca whined playfully.

Trey felt an odd choice suddenly looming. Then he decided to take a chance even crazier than going to the Ansel Mansion alone in the dark. He turned to Sam, who was sitting beside him, grabbed her by the side of the head, and kissed her hard on the mouth. Then he turned back to Becca and did the same. To his surprise, neither woman pulled away, nor did either say anything afterward, though they both looked at him with pleading eyes.

"I'll be okay," he lied. "Besides, seems like I've got a shot at a threesome if I make it back now."

Both women groaned and got out, slamming their doors. His joke worked, and he was pulling away before they had a chance to change their minds. As they went into Sam's house, Trey looked at them for what he knew would be the last time.

He parked in front of the gate and stared at the house again. He hadn't ever really left this place, he realized. Not after he had fallen through the floor while retrieving Ansel's journal. It was like he was trapped, wandering the burnt and broken halls, trying hundreds of doors that would lead to freedom from this nightmare.

When Trey had been here before, one of the

doors seemed to open up to the 1800s. While he had tried to pass it off as an impossible hallucination at the time, he was now sure that it held the answer. He would have to hope that he could find his way to the Winslow house in the past, and then, even more impossibly, find his way back to the present.

He laughed as he killed the engine and climbed out into the icy darkness. It sounded almost as ridiculous as a giant worm turning kids into dolls.

The gate was frozen shut. Trey had to warm the latch with his breath for several minutes before he could get it to budge. Then the gate was squealing open, and he was inside the grounds. The cold only barely masked the smell of burnt wood and rotting leaves. Trey tried not to look at the looming trees or even the fountain that rose out of the fog in front of him. Instead, he kept his focus on the ground to make sure that he didn't trip on his way in.

When he reached the front stairs, he turned on his flashlight and made his ascent. The wood groaned in recognition of his steps as if to welcome him home. Once he was inside, the darkness became oppressive, and the air seemed colder, even without the presence of the fog.

Previously, he had been transported to the past when opening the front door from the inside, so he tried that first. He couldn't decide if he was annoyed or relieved when he realized that everything he could see through the fog looked the same.

"Come on, you haunted fucker," he whispered.

"Hello?" a voice from behind him asked.

Trey jumped with a faint shout. He started to turn while reaching into his coat for his gun. His light fell upon an unfamiliar form that had been standing inside the foyer.

25

Henrietta hadn't slept as well that night as she had hoped. In her dreams, she saw Hyrum swinging from a tree while maggots poured from his face. When she tried to get closer to him, she realized that she was hanging herself. The boy Malthus was watching her from a distance, painting a doll that looked just like her.

When she awoke, she was drenched in so much sweat that it felt as if her sheets were swimming around her. She lifted her bedding up and saw a mass of white undulating all over her.

"God in heaven!" she cried as she fell to the ground.

The maggots spilled out across the floorboards, where they tried to sink into the cracks to the earth beneath. Still screaming, Henrietta pulled her nightgown off and cast it aside. The maggots still clung to her skin, from her breasts to her groin. She clawed at her skin to remove them, but could never get them all. It wasn't until she finally collapsed, sobbing, that she realized she was naked with Joshua still in the house. For some reason, the boy hadn't woken from her cries.

Forcing herself to stand on shaky legs, she grabbed enough clothing to cover herself from her son and went to fetch a pail to wash the maggots away. She would have to look under the house for some animal carcass, she guessed, though the lack of flies last night was odd indeed for this many of the grave worms to find their way inside.

As she started rinsing the floor, she realized that she hadn't noticed his recently unkempt hair poking out from under her son's blankets. Her heart hammered in her chest as panic overtook her for the second time that morning. Henrietta threw the sheet off his bed to find it empty. He had gone somewhere in the night.

"No! No! No!" she screamed.

Not even taking time to dress properly, she threw open the door and barreled outside. It didn't look like they had bothered to replace her guard after the mob went after Winslow. She cursed to herself. If they had, perhaps Joshua would've been kept in last night.

The town was quiet. The sun was just beginning to creep over the horizon, bathing everything amid the trees in a bluish twilight. Though it was summer, an unnatural cold crept into her bones, causing her to shiver uncontrollably. She tried not to think of the feeling of white worms wiggling against her skin.

Like a madwoman, she tore through the town, still barefoot and with only the smallest stitch of clothing. No matter where she looked, there was no sign of her boy anywhere. She looked in windows, under shrubs, and called his name down every street. No one came out to help her. No one yelled for her to be quiet. She was truly, completely, alone.

Finally, her eyes fell on the forest. It was happening again. Even with Hyrum Winslow dead, it was happening again. Henrietta ran headlong into the woods in the direction that would take her to the Winslow home. She knew that Joshua was somewhere between here and there, and she had to get to him before it was too late.

Hours seemed to pass in a blur as she ran through the twilight forest. Her feet bled from dozens of cuts, and her undergarments were torn in multiple places. Eventually, she slipped in a patch of mud and slid down an embankment to a small stream that wound between gnarled roots. The water was ice that flayed the skin from her bones. She shivered and clutched her knees to her chest, rocking back and forth. Her ankle was twisted and too swollen to walk.

"Joshua!" she called, but her voice was hoarse.

Only then did she realize that she hadn't stopped yelling for him since she entered the woods. Her voice finally gave out, and she clutched the roots of the nearest tree, sobbing.

"Please, Lord," she whispered. "Please. Not Joshua. You've already taken Ezekiel and Willard from me. Not Joshua, too. Please, Jesus Christ. Please."

As she lay there shivering, she watched as her blood mingled with the mud in the stream before it vanished between the roots of the tree. This gave words to a different prayer.

"Rootmother. Green Goddess, I beseech ye," she said. "Lead me from this place so that I may know what has become of my son. Khythk'uhn. She Who Sleeps Beneath the Trees. Heed my prayer."

How she knew these names for the heathen goddess of this forest, she knew not, but no sooner did the words leave her mouth than she felt a renewed vigor. Though it was agonizing to walk on her swollen ankle, she pressed on. Though it was madness, it seemed that the forest itself was leading her somewhere, as there was now a path set before her, where the trees, ferns, and scrub brush did not grow. She wound through the forest on this fresh walkway until she arrived at a gathering of black boulders that jutted out of the ground. Her eyes struggled to focus on the stones, causing her to look away.

That was when she noticed that she was outside the remains of the Ansel Mansion. Pulled on like Moses through the desert, Henrietta limped around the wall to the front gate of the house. She pushed her way inside those pearly gates and continued her journey past the beautiful fountain and up the steps. When she reached the top, she was nearly delirious, but she knew that salvation lay beyond. The door swung inward, and she stumbled inside.

Inside, the house should have been dark, save for the thin beams of light that filtered in through the windows, yet ornate chandeliers and candelabras bathed her in a warm glow. Even half-destroyed as it was, Henrietta had never seen such majesty in all her days. The ornate woodwork still shone as if it had been polished that very morning. Marble pillars with gold filigrees adorned the ends of the sweeping stair-cases that led to the floors above.

It was magnificent.

Then she slipped on mud that she herself had tracked in and cracked her head upon the floor, sending her spiraling into darkness.

26

"Hello?" the woman called out again. "I need help."

As she stepped out of the darker shadows, Trey felt his stomach drop. This woman could have passed for the mother of the Winslow kid. She wore what looked to be a white undergarment, like he would have expected from the 1800s. Her dark hair was a mess of mud and sticks, while a faint trickle of blood marred her pale face. Clearly, Trey, or at least someone dressed like him, was not what the woman expected to see. The woman seemed to recoil from him just as soon as she was close enough to really see him.

"W-who are you?" she stammered.

"Treyton Savage…uh…ma'am," he answered.

This had certainly not been what he had expected either, but something told him that this was his only chance at stopping this nightmare, so he needed to figure out who this woman was before she bolted.

"Can we step outside?" he asked. "It's not safe in this old house."

The woman gave him a curt nod and followed him back into the night. Now came the hard part. How was he going to explain to her that she had been *Back to the Future*'d?

"I'm sure this is very confusing for you—" he began.

"Why are you dressed like that?" she interrupted. "I've seen many queer things in Jackson Point, but nothing such as that."

Trey shifted uncomfortably from one foot to the other. The night air was bitingly cold, but he didn't think he could convince this woman to get into a 21st-century car yet.

"What year do you think it is, miss?" he asked, finally.

"It's 1906," she replied. "And you may call me Henrietta."

"Alright, Henrietta. This is going to be a shock to you, but you aren't in the year 1906 anymore. It's actually 2025. This house—the Ansel house—has a way of transporting people through time. In your case, over one hundred years."

"The Lord hates a liar," she whispered. "This is more heathen nonsense. You must be in league with Hyrum." Then her whole demeanor changed, and she stood straighter and more defiant. "You murderer!"

"Hyrum?" Trey asked, trying to ignore her anger. "Hyrum Winslow?"

She said nothing, but the slight change in her shoulders told him that he was on the right track.

"I don't know the man. He was killed by an angry mob in 1906 because children were going missing. That's as much as I know about the man —though I believe his family might be doing this all again."

The woman—Henrietta—didn't respond. Instead, she barreled past Trey, shoving him down the steps into the mud. By the time he was standing again, she had vanished past the gate and into the night.

"Fuck me," he said.

It didn't take him long to find her again.

Trey pulled up to the curb beside the time-lost woman, who had made it partway down Main Street before finally collapsing from shock. She was on her knees on the sidewalk, intermittently wailing or swaying side to side. While no one else was currently outside, Trey couldn't be certain that this would go unnoticed for much longer, so he killed the engine and tried to approach Henrietta as slowly as possible to prevent her from running away again.

"This isn't real," she said. "This isn't real. It's a dream. Just a dream. He killed my husband. He killed my boys. Now I'm in Hell. Why have you forsaken me, Lord? Where am I? It's just a dream. My boys. My Willard. Joshua. Ezekiel. He killed them. This isn't real…"

At first, Trey thought her babble was simply a response to the shock of being over one hundred years in her future, but then he noticed the names of those he figured were her husband and sons. Victims of Hyrum Winslow and Thy'ar. He crouched in front of her and gently placed his hands on her shoulders.

"Henrietta?" he asked. "What happened to your boys? To your husband? What happened to Joshua, Ezekial, and Willard?"

"He killed them," she repeated, not looking at him. "He killed them and replaced them with little dolls. Little dolls of my boys. Of my husband. Even after they hung him, he still killed Joshua. His own children, too. He is a monster."

"I'm so sorry," Trey said. "I know this is overwhelming, but I need you to get into my car. It isn't safe out here."

Though she didn't respond, the shattered woman allowed him to lead her to his car. He sat her in the passenger seat and closed the door. If she had any thoughts about the modern vehicle, she didn't show it. Rather, she continued to mutter to herself as she stared out the window that her ragged breath had started to fog up.

Trey got back into the driver's seat and turned on the defrost. As the warm air began to circulate, the windows cleared again, and the beleaguered podcaster started to drive. The pair had two destinations tonight, and only one of them he knew how to get to.

"Henrietta," he said softly. "I need your help. Whatever happened a hundred years ago to your family, it's happening again, but I have a plan to stop it. I need to know how to get to the Winslow house. The layout of Jackson Point is the same as it was in your time. Do you think that you can guide me there?"

"This place is wrong," she whispered. "The buildings. The lights. This carriage. It's all so wrong. What year did you say it was?"

"2025. It's February. I honestly couldn't tell you the day, though it doesn't really mean much here."

"It should be July the 5th," she said. "It should be 1906."

"I know," Trey said as he turned down Murder Creek. "Time is different here. Have you heard of the Green Goddess? The Rootmother?"

"Local superstition," she answered, her voice growing stronger.

Outside, the trees loomed over them, cutting through the fog like broken bones.

"That's the thing, she, *it*, isn't just superstition. She's real, and she's the reason time doesn't work here. She's the reason you walked into that house in 1906 and back out into 2025. She's the reason all of this is happening, or her spawn is."

"A demon?" Henrietta asked.

"Something like that," Trey replied. "Someone has been taking people again and leaving dolls behind. I did some research, and it led me to the name Hyrum Winslow. There's something else… a kid that, well, that dresses like you, like he stumbled out of 1906 has been running around town, taunting us. I think he must be one of the Winslow boys."

"Malthus."

"Sure. Sure. Anyway, I think we need to go to their house and destroy it—the *thing* doing this, and possibly Malthus or whoever he is, as well. Will you help me?"

She was quiet again for a long time. When

she finally turned to look at Trey, her eyes were flint.

"Yes," she said. "I wish to send that whole family back to hell. This isn't the way to their house, however."

"No, it's not," Trey said. "A friend left something here for me that I think we'll need."

He pulled into the driveway of the abandoned house that he was pretty sure Nancy Tench had been hiding in. It was possible that this whole thing was a trap, but he needed to take that chance.

"Stay here," Trey told Henrietta.

She didn't protest.

He left the car running and pulled out his gun and flashlight. Like before, the door swung ajar, moving faintly from the night breeze. Trey swallowed hard and pressed inside.

Inside the house seemed mostly unchanged. The smell of piss and shit was covered by a dampness from the fog that made it a little more tolerable. Trey still had no idea exactly what he was looking for. Something Nance thought would help him against Thy'ar.

What could kill a giant worm? He wondered. *Maybe she left me a bigass bird.*

Nothing was amiss in the front room, so he worked his way back to the kitchen, where he assumed she had been sleeping. His light passed over the rotten food and overturned table before settling on a pile of fertilizer bags. Beside the bags were several cans of what he expected to be diesel, and a few road flares on top.

"Son of a bitch," Trey said. "She wants me to use a bomb?"

He walked over and inspected the bags. Ammonium Nitrate Fertilizer was printed on each. Upon closer inspection, Trey realized that what he had mistaken for road flares were actually something else. Something with fuses sticking out of the end. Dynamite. The explosives looked incredibly old, and he wasn't sure that they would even detonate, but it was worth a shot.

A small note was scribbled on a piece of paper tucked in with the bags. It read:

Seal the tunnel. That's all we can do for now.

How does she know? He thought.

Trey looked back over the supplies. He had a rough idea of how this would work based on a case he did an episode on once that involved a makeshift bomb at a courthouse. The perpetrator had combined fertilizer with diesel and ignited it with a smaller explosive that he had obtained elsewhere. The results had been catastrophic. If this worked, he wasn't sure about killing Thy'ar, but it would certainly bring down the house around them. Gingerly, he picked up the dynamite and set it on the counter. They didn't detonate, so that was good. Putting his gun away first, Trey shouldered a bag of fertilizer and returned to the car.

After a few minutes of hauling everything out, the car was a moving bomb. Now he just needed to get to their target.

"Which way?" he asked as he climbed back into the driver's seat.

27

S am and Becca huddled together on the couch, neither one willing to break the silence that had hung over them since they let Trey go. The idea seemed worse and worse as the night wore on with no word from him. Sam started to fear that he was already dead; that they would find a porcelain doll of him on her doorstep come morning. As annoying as he had been lately, she felt a hollow pit forming in her stomach. That kiss hadn't been as repulsive as she would have thought. Neither did she feel jealous that he had kissed Becca right afterward.

What is happening to me? She thought. *This has to be the craziest rebound in history.*

Becca gently nuzzled into her neck. That felt nice. Samantha also enjoyed being the other woman's comfort. She felt best being the strong one, the leader. Becca needed her now, more than ever, and, selfish as it felt to admit, Sam liked that.

"We have to go after him," Becca whispered.

Sam had been thinking the same for the last little bit. Brave, or stupid, as he was, Trey shouldn't be handling this alone. They never should have let him go. *Sam* never should have let him go.

"I'll grab his keys," Sam said, standing. "You grab blankets and fill up some water bottles. We might not be coming back tonight."

After grabbing Trey's spare keys from a drawer in the kitchen, Sam decided to start the car now so the pair didn't freeze their asses off. Her hand was on the doorknob just as it turned on its own accord. The door suddenly flung inwards, knocking Sam off balance. Head spinning, she skittered back from the open door, reaching for her gun.

A heavy boot kicked her in the hand, snapping her wrist just as the pistol was pulled free. It skittered across the floor and under the couch.

"Becca, run!" she shouted.

Only then did she look up to see who had finally come for them. Deputy Granger loomed over her, his sidearm pointed at her face. His once soft expression had been replaced with something altogether alien. It was clear that he no longer saw her as anything but an obstacle.

"Drop the gun, Clarence," Becca said coolly from the hall.

Sam looked over her shoulder to see Becca pointing a shotgun at Granger. He simply smiled.

"I'll shoot your dark friend here before you can squeeze that trigger, *Rebecca*," he said. Sam noticed his voice was uneven, as was the cadence of his speech. He seemed to be racing from one word to the next. "I've returned from the dead once, don't think I can't do it again. Set that down slowly, or her brains'll be all over this floor."

Becca did as she was asked. With a quick flick of his wrist, Granger motioned both women back into the front room. They sat together on the couch while he remained standing, his gun slowly drifting from woman to woman.

"You died," Sam said. "We saw you die. Gutted by that *thing*."

"You didn't see what you thought you did, sister."

"Drop the racist cop act," Becca hissed. "What the fuck, Clarence? You're one of them?"

The deputy seemed to shift nervously, like he

was waging some internal battle. The bad cop seemed to win out, and he was ice cold again.

"I was born into it, Becca. Never had no choice. My…membership was kept a secret from most, so that I could ensure the sheriff and her cousin toed the line. When he made too much trouble, I took care of him."

Sam felt the world fall out from under her. All this time, they had been tricked by this psychopath. And that meant Gideon hadn't been the one to kill Arthur…

"I call bullshit," Becca continued. "Sam and Trey told me his fucking head was ripped off. You saying you did that?"

His hand tightened on the grip of his pistol.

"You want me to show you?" he growled.

"Why?" Sam asked. "Why even tell us about the dolls and Mary Simmons? Any of it?"

"Because I needed to lure Tench back into the open, and I think I finally did. Fuck! It's too loud!" He rubbed his temple with his free hand, his face twisted in pain. Then he was normal again. "Now, where's Savage?"

Sam's mind raced. She needed to keep him talking until they came up with something. But what could they even do?

"We don't know," she said. "He went out to look for the Winslow House, but that was hours ago."

"They were very clear," he said. "I'm to kill all of you, but Tench is my priority. If he isn't back in the next five minutes, I'll kill both of you cunts and go find him myself. Then he can take me to Tench and—"

She knew this might be the only opening they would have, so she risked showing their hand.

"Evelyn McReedy is dead," she proclaimed. "Shot through the head tonight. Did you know that?"

A look of shock passed over Granger's face for a fleeting moment.

"Bullshit," he hissed. "I just spoke to her today."

"Looks like Tench got there just after you, then," Becca added.

The cords in his neck bulged, but he slumped down into Sam's favorite chair. His eyes never left the pair, even as his gun drooped slightly.

"I was supposed to find her before she could do anything," he whispered. His voice was cracking, and his words jumbling together again. "She'll never forgive me for letting one of the elders die..."

Sam felt her shirt sticking to her back. She needed to keep stalling as long as possible. But to what end? There was no way she could get to the gun under the couch in time.

"Why now, Granger? Why is the Fifth Signet risking this all now?"

His eyes grew distant, as if he was looking past them rather than at them. His gun drooped even further. Now the barrel was aimed at their legs rather than their chests.

"Tench. We knew she was doing something. Sightings, break-ins," he said. "It was only a matter of time before she did something...like this. So I was instructed to make both problems go away, no matter the risk."

"That's why you called in the order for Ron?" she pressed.

"Yeah," he mumbled. "We knew what we could wake up in the Winslow House if the time was right."

"So you woke up the worm just to get us?" Becca asked.

Sam could feel the other woman's legs tighten like springs. She was preparing to jump at the man.

"Her children all must wake for the end to come," he whispered. "Korshalum has always wandered these woods, communed with the faithful, but Thy'ar and the others sometimes sleep like their mother. Why does this hurt so much? It's only supposed to harm the weak."

Then his eyes refocused, and his grip on the gun tightened again. Some internal struggle was ended, yet again. Sam noticed, but unfortunately, Becca did not.

"Becca, no!" Sam shouted, but it was too late.

The other woman sprang at the deputy, and he pulled the trigger, causing the house the fill with thunder.

28

Trey was finally looking at the source of all of this madness: the Winslow House. It was large, with a facade of broken windows. A blue door with an ornate window hung ajar—the knob and part of the frame had been torn loose by something. In the front yard, an old, broken-down car was rotting in the grass. All things considered, the house looked far newer than it should have.

"Are you sure this is it?" Trey asked. "This doesn't look old enough."

"It doesn't look the same, but the shape is right. This is the house. I can feel it."

"Alright. Let's get the stuff inside."

She was wearing his coat, but the poor woman was still barefoot and nearly naked. Still, Trey needed help carrying in all of the fertilizer before someone or some*thing* found them. Inside, the house was a mix of old and older. The floors looked like hundred-year-old hardwood that hadn't been maintained, but the peeling wallpaper reminded him of his grandmother's house. It smelled like wet dirt, but nothing fouler. Henrietta looked around as the light of Trey's flashlight passed over the foyer.

"This is it," she said quietly. "I've been in this far. Somewhere is a basement, where Hyrum... worked."

"That tracks," Trey said.

She looked at him, confused.

"That makes sense," he corrected. "Thy'ar attacked me in a basement. It must have tunnels under the town."

She nodded, though he could tell that she still had no idea what the hell he was talking about. They carried everything into the foyer and left it there until Trey came up with a plan on what to actually do with it. As they began checking doors for one that led downstairs, they heard a loud thump overhead, followed by a bout of laughter. Children's laughter.

"Malthus," Henrietta hissed.

Trey pulled his gun back out and headed for the large staircase. This part of the home had been largely left original: an ornate staircase in the central room curved up to a landing beyond.

It wasn't unlike the one in the Ansel Mansion, Trey realized, if a bit smaller. The pair crept up the stairs as quietly as the squeaky boards allowed.

At the landing, Trey cast his light down one hallway and then the other. There was no sign of the boy. Then he saw it: a writhing pile of maggots just at the edge of his light. He pointed at the graveworms, and to his surprise, Henrietta simply walked toward them. Trey quickly followed, his pulse racing. They were being taken away from the basement for a reason.

As they got closer, the white threads began to undulate more ferociously, as if they were trying to move as one solid mass. Just as Henrietta got an arms-length away, the pile of maggots rose into the air some four feet, and took on a vaguely human shape. Only then did Henrietta scream, and it was a cry of grief, not of fear.

The maggots had formed a boy, but not the one Trey had come to know as Malthus.

"Joshua," she sobbed. "What has happened to you?"

The boy laughed and barreled past the pair, shoving Trey aside. Trey turned and leveled his pistol at the kid's back. Whether it looked like her son or not, it had just been a mass of worms, which meant it wasn't human.

"No!" Henrietta cried, knocking Trey's arm aside.

His shot went wild, blowing apart one of the newel posts at the top of the stairs. As Henrietta ran past him, he grabbed her by his coat to stop her. She slipped right out and continued on as if nothing had happened.

"Joshua! Wait!"

"Henrietta, don't!" Trey called after her. "It's not your son!"

It was no use. All of her righteous anger had faded away, replaced by maternal instinct to protect her son. She was down the stairs and around the corner faster than Trey thought was possible, especially in the darkness of the house. He cursed and followed after her, hoping that it wouldn't be too late by the time he finally caught up to her.

At the bottom of the stairs, he lost sight of her and the boy. A door slammed to his right. Trey ran that direction, ending up within sight of the foyer. A large ornate cherry wood door loomed in front of him.

This wasn't here before, he thought.

Trey looked around in mild panic as he realized that the house no longer looked like a combination of dated architectural styles. Though still dark, the house was once again firmly in the

1800s, looking as it must have when Hyrum Winslow had called it home.

A few months ago, he had just been a podcaster. Now he needed to be something more. Someone who was ready to risk his life for a relative stranger. Trey opened the door, filling the room around him with light. Stone steps led down into the earth, polished as if they had only recently been installed. Kerosene lamps were set in sconces every few feet on both sides, bathing the stairwell in amber.

Just like last October, the forces that moved through Jackson Point were leading him. Trey didn't like feeling like being a pawn in some cosmic game, but what choice did he have? What choice did any human have against the Elder Ones? All he could hope was that Henrietta would be at the bottom of these stairs, alive.

With one final, steadying breath, Trey descended into the bowels of Jackson Point.

29

It couldn't be Joshua. It couldn't be. And yet it looked just like him. It ran just like him. It laughed just like him. So Henrietta couldn't stop until she caught him.

At the bottom of the stairs, she found a large wooden door with a recessed slat in the center. It seemed as if it could slide open for the occupant of the basement to look out. This must have been Hyrum's workshop, and no doubt he had installed a door such as this to prevent his family or servants from barging in on his wicked work. Even though her hands shook, she tried the door. It held fast.

Then the slat opened with a faint click.

"What's the password?" Joshua asked.

Henrietta felt her eyes grow hot.

"Joshua, please," she begged.

"Password?"

The question stirred something in her memory, but she couldn't determine what. Her mind was still a jumble. She had somehow found herself in a different time, and that alone threatened to fracture what sanity she had left. Instead, she had chosen to ignore the strange surroundings of this future Jackson Point and instead focus on getting revenge for her family. So far, it had worked, but only just. Now, as she tried to think back to what seemed to be only a few months ago, she was confronted with her reality again.

Henrietta slumped against the wall as her chest began to tighten. The lights were different, the buildings larger, the carriage loud and fast. The clothing, the guns. It was all wrong. It couldn't be real. No, she was having a nightmare. Her boys were safe, and her Willard was beside her. The Winslow family was not wicked or cruel. They played in the rain. Joshua wouldn't let the others inside, wet as they were, without saying the password. Then she remembered.

"Towering pine," she said.

The eyes behind the slat vanished, and the door swung slowly inward. Henrietta stepped inside, and the door slammed shut behind her. Distantly, she thought she could hear Trey calling her name, asking her to come back to the surface, but he seemed so far away...

Inside was Hyrum's workshop, just as she had thought. Closest to the door was a floor of lacquered wood that shone faintly from the lamps. A lone workbench sat against the right-most wall. It was cluttered with paints and brushes. In the distance, the floor ended just before the light did, leaving a cavernous opening of dirt.

Worst of all, though, were the piles of dolls that towered to either side of her. None were painted yet. All stared at her with white, lidless eyes.

"Do you like it, mother?" Joshua asked, suddenly beside her.

Henrietta jumped. Then she realized how exposed her body was, and covered her chest with her arms. She suddenly felt so vulnerable.

"Malthus brought us here, Ezekiel and I," he said. "It was a wonderful thing to join them."

"Join them?" she asked.

His face was wrong. It looked like her boy, but the eyes were glassy, just like the dolls. Suddenly, the boy shifted, and for a moment, he was a pillar of maggots again, shimmering before taking the shape of Ezekiel. Henrietta covered her mouth to stifle a scream before stumbling backward.

"Yes," Ezekiel said. "We are all inside, now."

Then it shimmered again, and it was Malthus.

The boy looked like he always did, though his once vacant expression was now one of malice.

"What did you do to my boys?" she asked, her anger returning.

"The same as I did to my mother. My brother. My sister. The other children. The same as I will do to you in a few moments."

The boy turned and walked to the bench and grabbed a doll from amidst the brushes and pots of paint. He returned and placed it firmly in Henrietta's hands. She knew before even looking at it what she would see. The doll was painted to look just like her. Without a second glance, she dropped it to the floor where it shattered.

"Father was right about so many things," the boy said. "And wrong about so many more. He killed my sister Winnifred in a vain attempt at summoning Thy'ar. But the Scion of the End comes at no man's beck and call. Father realized that one sacrifice wasn't enough, so he created these." Malthus spread his arms, waving his fingers at the dolls like he was conducting an invisible choir. "He filled each with poor Winnie's blood, draining her over some weeks, I was told. Each effigy was to be painted to look like a citizen of the town and offered to The Grave Worm.

"As for a more substantial sacrifice, he planned to use his other children when the time was right. What he didn't know was that I had already joined the Great One, and there was no need for him any longer."

Henrietta felt her stomach turn as bile bit at the back of her throat. The ground beneath her feet had begun to shake, ever so slightly, and the smell of dirt had become mixed with rotten flesh.

"I am his harbinger, his prophet, his voice," Malthus continued. "Each absorbed adds to the Great One, but none holds the place of honor that I do." The boy bent down and picked up a shard of the broken Henrietta doll. "Pity, this one was my best work. Father never realized I held his skill with a brush. The dolls were useless to Thy'ar, but I found them amusing."

The rumbling grew much more potent, and a slithering sound filled the air. It was clear to her that something large was coming toward them from the darkness beyond the workshop, and she needed to get away. Henrietta turned and ran back to the door. She tried to pry it open, but it wouldn't budge. Through the slat, she could see Trey watching her with panicked eyes.

"The door!" he shouted. "Unlatch the door!"

But there was no lock that she could see. Futile as it was, she slammed her fists against the door again and again until they ached.

"Don't worry, Etty, we'll be together again, soon," Willard said from behind her.

She tried to ignore the thing that wasn't her husband, but a firm hand gripped her shoulder and turned her around. He was looming over her, his dead eyes staring. Then he was Eliza.

"Henrietta, darling," she cooed. "I wish I had listened to you. Hyrum is a bad man. He beats us something awful. I...I think he killed Winnie."

"Stop!" Henrietta shouted. "You are a monster, Malthus Winslow! Face me yourself."

Eliza shimmered, and maggots writhed. Then the dour little boy was staring up at her again.

"He is nearly here," the boy said. "He tunnels between her roots, waiting until his mother wakes. Then the end will come. Then I will rise in glory over a new world. One of pain."

Henrietta slapped the boy as hard as she could. His face became deformed for a moment, then the worms returned to their shape. Malthus began to laugh.

"Mother tried that as well," he said.

"Henrietta!" Trey called, sounding far off again. "You have to get out! It's here!"

Then the shaking became too much to ignore. In the darkness, something glistened. The slithering and shaking continued until the tunnel was filled with a pale bulk. It looked less like a maggot and more like a giant, misshapen slug. Its flesh was lumpy and covered with festering boils that oozed a thick, red substance. What seemed to be its head lacked eyes, but did have a round mouth filled with needle-like teeth. Henrietta felt her knees buckle. The last of her sanity began to crack at the sight of this abomination. In that instant, her faith in God wilted to nothing.

"Behold Thy'ar, Scion of the End, the Grave Worm, spawn of Khythk'uhn, She Who Sleeps Beneath the Trees," Malthus laughed. "You will join us, as will the rest of this town, and then she will wake. This will be pain like you have never imagined, Mrs. Frock."

Then a thick, mucous-covered appendage of the worm extended toward her. It was nearly translucent, revealing vessels of black and red blood flowing underneath. There was no escape for her. She knew in that instant that she was going to die. That left only one thing for her to do. Henrietta grabbed one of the kerosene lamps and threw it into Malthus before the boy could react. The fire engulfed him instantly, causing him to scream in a shrill voice as the maggots that made up his body sizzled and popped, filling the air with the foul smell of burning meat.

"Save me!" he cried. "Please! Father! Don't!"

Then the flaming pile could no longer retain its shape, and it collapsed onto the floor. Some of the maggots tried to escape, but the flames began to spread. Henrietta smiled just as the appendage of Thy'ar enveloped her. She felt her body dissolving. It was agony.

This is how my boys died, was the last thing that passed through her mind.

30

The bullet grazed Becca's thigh before exploding the pillow next to Sam. While the pain was worse than anything she had ever experienced before, her fight or flight instinct had full control. She slammed into him, knocking the chair over and causing his gun to fall. Then he threw her off like she weighed nothing, causing her to slam her head into the wall.

"You fucking bitch!" he shouted.

BANG. BANG. BANG.

Three shots rattled the house. Granger dropped to the floor again, crimson blossoming from his chest. Sam stood in front of the couch, a faint trail of smoke rising from the barrel of her revolver. Even though Becca's leg was hot and slick with blood, it was her head that hurt the most. She tried to shake the headache away before standing. Her legs felt like they would buckle from the attempt, but she still pulled herself up.

"You alright?" Sam asked.

"I'll survive," Becca replied.

"You haven't done anything," Granger gurgled.

Becca and Sam stood over him. His shirt was soaked red, while his lips were tinged with pink foam. Each ragged breath was punctuated by a hollow wheeze.

"This wasn't supposed to happen," he said. "I should have been protected. It was supposed to heal me."

"What the fuck are you talking about?" Sam asked.

His eyes already seemed to be struggling to focus. Becca wasn't even sure if he could see them anymore. Granger's breathing became shallower, and she was sure that he was going to pass at any moment. Then his head snapped toward them, and his voice became steadier, even though his words continued to run into each other like he was learning to talk.

"Jackson Point is but one nexus. We have believers at every resting place around the globe, working to awaken the Elder Ones. One day soon, your world will end, and you won't even know which god woke first."

Then the deputy began to convulse. His entire body shook violently, as if his death was being heralded by a seizure. That was when Becca noticed the smell; hidden under the coppery scent of blood and the acrid smoke of gunpowder, something wet and rotten was filling the air. It reminded her of spoiled milk. His shaking continued for a few more moments before he went still.

"What the fuck was that?" Becca asked.

"I don't—" Sam began. "Jesus Christ! Look at his face!"

Something, or several somethings, more accurately, were wriggling out of his nostrils and the corners of his eyes. It looked like small tentacles, the color of mayonnaise, were trying to break free of Granger's head. Becca felt her stomach turn, and in that moment, the pain in her head and her leg seemed farther away than ever. She limped over and retrieved the shotgun. When she returned, part of Granger's face was missing as whatever the tentacles were connected to began to burst free.

Becca blew Granger's head apart with a squeeze of the trigger.

Chunks of gore showered the room, including a few of the still writhing tentacles. Both women stared at the mess in silence until the movement stopped.

"My floor is fucked," Sam said.

They wrapped the body in garbage bags and dragged it to Trey's car. After Granger was loaded up, they took the time to clean Becca's leg. It still burned, but by now the bleeding had stopped. Before they left, the pair cleaned up the blood as best they could and placed Sam's favorite chair over the hole in the floor. It wasn't likely that any of this would matter at this point, but they didn't know what else to do.

Finally, they got into the car and started driving. For the first thirty minutes, they drove in circles around the town as neither of them had any idea where a safe place to hide a body was. In all this time, they still hadn't spoken of the thing that was trying to wriggle its way out of Granger's brain. By what must have been the tenth lap around Jackson Point, Becca decided to speak up.

"Let's go back to the house where we think Nancy was hiding," she said. "Maybe they'll blame it on her."

"Yeah…" Sam whispered.

Becca tried not to let her mind linger on the

image of the man dying on the floor; of his head exploding into a red mist from her gun. She failed spectacularly.

"What do you think that was?" Becca asked.

"I don't know," Sam answered. "Another *child*? Maybe whatever was inside Gideon. I don't know. He seemed to think it would protect him."

"Maybe it's what made him strong enough to rip Arthur's head off?"

"Maybe."

A few more minutes of silence passed.

"Do you think there are more of them?" Becca asked.

"Yeah," Sam said with a shudder. "Unfortunately, I do."

They stopped talking for good that time, until they pulled in front of the house. Sam took the legs and Becca the shoulders, and they carried Clarence Granger to his final resting place. They dropped him with a wet crunch in the bathtub and closed the door.

"We should burn it," Becca whispered.

Sam nodded. They dug around the house until they found some lighter fluid and an old kitchen lighter. Back in the bathroom, Becca doused both the body and the walls with the liquid until the bottle was empty. Sam threw what dry books and paper they could find onto the body like a makeshift funeral pyre. Becca lit a roll of toilet paper and threw it into the room. The flames whooshed to life, racing up the walls and over the body. They closed the door and briskly walked back out to the car.

They didn't leave until they saw smoke rolling out of the open door.

31

Trey could do nothing to help Henrietta. He watched in horror as the woman was engulfed by the Grave Worm. She never even cried out as her flesh sloughed off and was absorbed by Thy'ar. He shuddered as he thought about her body reforming out of the maggots that had made up Malthus. Hopefully, now that the boy was dead, that part of this horror show was over.

He slumped against the door, listening to the slurping noises that the thing made as it dissolved the woman. Hopelessness washed over him, and he had to resist the urge to wretch. This was far more horrific than anything that happened last year.

At least she got some small revenge, he thought.

Then he remembered the fertilizer. Trey

peeked through the slat one final time to make sure that the worm hadn't left. It was still undulating its appendage over the place where Henrietta Frock had just been. He still had a chance to end this, once and for all.

Taking the steps two at a time, Trey raced back up to the surface where he had left the supplies for the bomb. Without wasting any time, he began tossing the bags down to the basement. Many of them tore and spilled the thick, brown granules, but he didn't slow. There was no time. Once the fertilizer was down, Trey grabbed the cans of diesel and raced back to the bottom, dragging as much of the fertilizer with him as he could. Just outside the door, Trey mixed the fuel and ammonium nitrate together into a thick paste. The smell was starting to make him light headed, so he was forced to cover his nose with his shirt for the last of it. When he was satisfied that he had done the best that he could, he stuck the two sticks of dynamite near the base of the door and lit the fuses.

"Tell your mom hi for me!" he shouted through the door.

As if the creature suddenly noticed him for the first time, the walls began to shake. In that moment, Trey realized he didn't have any idea how much time he had to get away.

"Fuck me," he whispered.

Then he sprinted up the stairs again, this time praying that he wasn't about to be vaporized. The earth around the entire house began to shake as Thy'ar pushed out of the workshop after new prey.

Trey made it to the front door when he was thrown through the air. His eardrums ruptured, and he felt his back had been burned. The podcaster-turned-bomb maker slammed into the ground just past his car, as burning pieces of debris landed all around him. He couldn't tell if the ground was still shaking or if it was the concussion and tinnitus making him feel off balance. Shakily, he pushed himself up and saw the flaming ruins of the Winslow House sinking into the earth.

He touched the side of his head and felt blood running from his ears. He hoped that the damage wasn't too severe. It would be hard to be a podcaster if he couldn't edit his audio, he figured. The thought made him laugh. All of the tension and fear and disgust melted away in that moment as he laughed while watching the flaming wreckage of that evil house get swallowed up by Jackson Point.

Over the ringing in his ears, he thought he heard someone say his name.

"Trey!" they called again. This time, he was sure of it, even though they sounded distant.

He turned to see Nancy Tench standing over him. She pulled him to his feet and wrapped him in a jacket.

"We need to talk," he thought she said.

Trey nodded before passing out.

32

They heard the explosion from across town. Sam rolled the windows down to make sure that what she had heard wasn't in her imagination. There was no follow-up to the initial thunder-like crack, but the sky in the distance began to glow. Just as it did behind them.

"Trey," they both said at once.

Sam stepped on the accelerator and turned them toward Wacum Road—her best guess for where the glow was coming from. Beside her, Becca was tense. Sam took one hand off the wheel and grabbed Becca's thigh. Neither wanted to say what they were thinking. She tried to focus on the road; they had to get there before the volunteer fire department or the remaining deputies were rounded up. If Trey was still alive, they couldn't let the Fifth Signet get to him first, not anymore.

After a few minutes, the fire became much clearer through the trees. The road twisted around to a clearing where the half-sunken remains of a house crackled and belched out new flames. Sam's car sat at the edge of the property, covered in ash and broken boards. There was no sign of Trey.

"I didn't bring my other keys," she said. "We'll have to leave it."

"I don't see him, Sam," Becca cried. "Where is he?"

"We've gotta get home and grab his computer."

"I don't see Trey!"

"He's dead!" Sam shouted. "He probably saved our lives, Becca! We can't wait around and throw that away. Hold it together, at least until we're somewhere safe."

Becca started quietly sobbing, but she didn't remove Sam's hand. Sam turned around and fled back down the road toward town, hoping that they could still avoid notice. Her car, sitting there, was an issue, but she could claim that Trey took it without permission. They would say that he took the car and ran off after a fight. Maybe they'd buy it. She doubted it.

They pulled back into town. Already, there

was a flurry of activity as other cars raced past them to head down Wacum. The town firetruck followed with its siren blaring. In the distance, the other fire was also coloring the horizon. She wasn't sure Jackson Point had ever dealt with two fires at once before. She hoped that they could get them under control before the entire forest was a conflagration. So far, no one seemed to pay them any mind. Hopefully, they just assumed that the pair was curious about the explosion.

Sam turned onto Main Street and headed for her house when the other car ran her off the road. She slammed on the brakes just in time to stop them from crashing into a telephone pole. To her surprise, it was Becca who had a gun in her hand first. The other woman had her door open and was pointing the weapon over the roof of the car before Sam had even registered what had happened.

This fucking town, she thought.

"Stay back!" Becca shouted.

"I-I need help," the man from the other car stammered. His voice was shaky. He sounded young.

Sam opened her door and looked at him. In the faint light, she could see that he looked to be college-aged. He was wearing dirty clothes and sported a ragged beard from days without shaving. Though he had his hands up over his head, he was clutching a tattered leather notebook for dear life.

"Who are you?" Sam asked. "Why'd you try and run us off the road?"

"My name is Alex," he said. "Alex Ruiz-Cruz. I came looking for Treyton Savage. I listened to his podcast. Only he can help me."

Sam rocked back on her heels. His stupid plan had worked. Though that meant it had trapped this poor fucker here just like they had been trapped. Had Trey considered that?

"Trey's dead," she said. "If you really need help, follow us."

Without waiting for an answer, Sam climbed back into the car. After Becca was back inside, they were driving back down Main and turning off down the street to Sam's house.

"Why do you think we can trust this guy?" Becca asked.

"Trey would've," she answered. "Don't laugh."

Becca chewed on her lip and looked out the window.

❦

Back inside her house, Sam made coffee for Alex and sat him down in the chair over the bloody hole. Becca never took her eyes off the kid, her gun sitting on her lap. After handing him the mug, Sam grabbed Trey's laptop and set it on the coffee table. They still weren't safe here, so this would have to be quick. She opened the master file for the podcast.

"Tell us what you know about *Backwoods Grindhouse*," she said.

Her finger hovered over the delete button.

9 781951 138226